VILLAINS IN THE ROOM

VILLAINS IN THE ROOM

NEEYOPE™ BOOK ONE

VIZIER VAUGHN

www.khpublishers.com

"You can't change the whole world, just put your positive parts
into it, then let it go."

-Vizier Vaughn

CHAPTER 1

COMING TO AMERICA

In the heart of Manhattan's Upper East Side, from between the glass doors held by the doorman, emerges a Caribbean-Bajan migrant beauty named Meshel. She has a creamy caramel complexion wavy hairdo, confident and beautiful, the girl-turned-woman as she strides thru smoke-filled gritty Manhattan-New York City streets over the subways. As she struts, her hips naturally swing past some of the clothing boutiques while turning many heads. She turns and enters her favorite local eatery to order two large cups of Colombian dark-roast coffee. She walks into her favorite bookstore and browses through the latest edition of Essence magazine. *I'm out of time again, and the line is too long for me to pay right now.* She ponders further. *I think I'll return to this bookstore later.*

Hastening to leave, she stops at the crosswalk, as she will only cross streets at the crosswalk. She has an innate fear of being hit by cars. Meshel ignores the whistles of the construction crew's men having lunch. As she crosses the street onto the next corner, some more admirers give compliments, and some offer free rides in their cars. The fruit-vendor man smiles brightly at Meshel from behind his table of dragon fruit, desert cactus fruit, mangosteens, persimmons, and many fruits of paradise. She carefully smells some ripe mangoes, then she picks up a smaller purple coated mangosteen fruit to sample the taste; the succulent white fleshy fruit intrigues her taste buds.

Meshel is now grown in body, mind, and spirit. Emerging for her time to shine in her new environment, her new place living in America. Just as she emerged from between the glass doors of the building she works in, with the doorman's help, she came into her own through lessons she learned from old friends, relatives, new friends, and strange acquaintances. She returns to the same glass doors opened again by the doorman. She offers him one of the Colombian coffees, which he gladly accepts. They developed that rapport, and she has the reputation of always helping others with her best efforts. She sits back at work and slices one of the mangoes; the smell of mangoes causes her to reminisce on her childhood, the place from which she grew up in Barbados in the Caribbean. Wow, this mango tastes so good. I wish I had some steamed fish or fish cakes right now. Meshel can't help herself, and she begins to reminisce about her life as a child growing up in Barbados.

CHAPTER 2

LITTLE MESHEL

From her special space under the wooded foundation of her mother's house, Little Meshel looked out at the numerous trees, hills, and valleys of neighboring communities from her town in Barbados. She often wondered, why was I meant to be poor? She wore no frill clothing, was constantly adorned with hand-me-downs, and her best shoes were repeats from her eldest sister Estelle. It was a fortunate coincidence that they wore the same size at different ages.

Meshel and Estelle had different fathers. Meshel's father was a handsome and relatively tall man, his parents migrated with him and his siblings, an older brother and two sisters, to Barbados from Grenada when he was still a baby. His genetics blessed him with above-average body proportions that came together very well. Meshel's physique was reminiscent of her Grenadian aunts. She had sculpted, voluptuous breasts, a slim waist, a pretty face, and strong hands and feet. She was a beauty for eyes to see.

Meshel's beauty wasn't complemented by nice clothing. However, her quick wit more than made up for her lack of material possessions. She had a sharp analytical mind and an even sharper tongue. She didn't mince her words, and compromise was not her forte. But life would eventually teach her about compromise.

Meshel grew up in a house her mother owned. Their home was bare-bones and worn; inside, they were missing a few doors and windows. Despite the lack of affluence, Meshel's mother, Celine, still managed to own a washing machine. Celine was obsessed with ensuring all the clothes and linen were washed properly and smelled good. Lack of fancy clothing didn't mean her children had to be presented as downtrodden.

Meshel was a hard worker like her mother and gave one hundred percent to anything she cared about. She believed in earning the right to have the best for herself and those closest to her. Her frustration would manifest whenever she dealt with anyone who settled for mediocrity or slacked in their work ethic. Her grandmother, Brownie, a religious woman, would urge Meshel to control her anger. She would often say to Meshel, "When you get mad, take three sips of some water and turn to the east!"

"Why to the east?" Meshel asked.

"Because that's the way to New Jerusalem Mammi daughter."

Brownie's advice stuck with her throughout her life, and Meshel often needed six or more sips of water to deal with some of her friends.

CHAPTER 3

CELINE

Meshel's mother, Celine, was a modest yet attractive woman. Her children called her "Mammi." She dressed in simple clothing and kept her nails and hair clean. She carried herself with grace and dignity and appeared content with her modest life. However, she was sure to exhibit strength in her presence through her words. She spoke boldly, with authority, and often embarrassed others when she needed to get her point across. Her words were often blunt and brash. She was determined to teach her daughters to be clean women who maintained their dignity while having the courage to speak up for themselves.

Celine's legacy included her ability to deliver an unfiltered description of whatever her children did to upset her. She often scolded her sons, "Oh, you think you're a man now because you see the foam when you pee?!" She also gave a good tongue lashing to her daughters, "Oh, you think you're a woman? You're smelling yourself now?" The list of Mammi's verbal blows go on and on. Mammi even accosted her younger brother Greg once after one of his many female exploits came to her house asking for him, "Greg! Who do you think you are, King Cock?"

Celine was under-educated, and aside from her sharp tongue, she felt she didn't have the intellect to carry herself far in life. However, she was determined to ensure that her daughters pursued a higher level of academics.

CHAPTER 4

BROWNIE

Grandma Brownie was Celine's mother and her first influence in life. As her nickname indicated, Brownie had a dark brown deep chocolate brownie complexion. Brownie was the daughter of Ethiopian immigrants, and her husband was the son of Irish and Portuguese immigrants. They were both second-generation immigrants to the island of Barbados in the Caribbean. Brownie's husband loved, cherished, and provided everything for her. She loved him and cared for all they had, including their six children.

Brownie proclaimed to be a devout Christian, although she did not attend church frequently. Nonetheless, she carried many values and traditions from her faith. She often sang her favorite spiritual hymn while alone or with her grandchildren:

> *"Oh, this world is not my home. I'm just passing through.*
> *And if heaven is not my home, then Lord, what will I do?*
> *Oh, the angels beckon me from heaven's open doors.*
> *And I can't feel at home in this world anymore."*

Brownie often used the term of endearment, "Mammi's daughter," to refer to her granddaughters and "Son-Son" for her grandsons. Whichever grandchild she was engaged with at any particular moment, it didn't matter; she generalized these terms. Perhaps she was overwhelmed by the many grandchildren, or old age caught up to her. Either way, her grandchildren felt the warmth of her love.

Known by her grandchildren for holding on strongly to her faith, Brownie was fulfilled as she believed that her greatest success was teaching them about her faith. She feared greatly that her grandkids would be 'cat-spraddled' into the world's chaos of unbelief and half-truths. Her grandchildren never knew her to waiver in her faith in God until her untimely death.

Brownie was calm and peaceful, and she lived life with ease. Never making a big fuss over anything and always willing to help someone in need, Brownie died harboring the pain and anger she suffered at the hands of a friend turned enemy, whom she called a "vampire." This was the only time her grandchildren witnessed her express anger and rage.

When Brownie was 55 years old, she invited her girlfriend Eva to build a small hut within her parcel of land. This was supposed to be temporary, just for a time, until Eva was ready to buy her own land. However, Eva disproved Brownie's trust by manipulating the land title documents and transferring some of the land into her name.

"That Vampire!" Brownie screamed, "She can't walk when it's daytime, but she can fly at night!" Brownie cussed up a storm about "that deceitful-ingrate, Eva!" She was so distraught that she nearly lost her mental state. The hurt and pain of her friend's betrayal and theft almost left her on the opposite end of her faith.

CHAPTER 5

COOL RUNNINGS

It was cool runnings for Lemar. He was tucked away quietly under the shadow of an Elm tree overhanging from the Upper East Side of New York City's Central Park. He felt cooler on this hot summer day as he enjoyed licking the dripping cone of chocolate ice cream. He thought about his favorite ice cream flavor from his childhood, Jamaican grape-nut ice cream, created by Granny Mae from the hillsides near the capital city of Kingston. *Man, I loved the crunch of those grape-nuts in the ice cream*, he thought. This is where Lemar parked his work truck at lunchtime; just around the corner and a few blocks north was his favorite bookstore.

After cleaning up the chocolate ice cream streaks on his hand, Lemar headed back to his work truck and drove off to his next assigned destination. *There goes the bookstore*, he thought, driving by but heading much farther north to Harlem and then into Washington Heights, where he parks for his next job as an electrical systems repairman. Immediately he sees a lady, a Latina pushing her cart of flavored ices.

"Icy señor?" She asks Lemar.

"Yeah, let me have one with Tamarindo (tamarind)." He replies as he takes out a dollar bill to pay her. The day was still hot and dry, but the extra flavored ice was a cool welcome. Tasting the flavor of the tamarind brought Lemar back into his memories of past times growing up in Jamaica. Tamarinds were one of the fruits he picked directly off trees with his friends and family, as well as ackees, pimentos, and limes for sugar-water lime-ade. He remembered the pigeons cooing in cages, the goats crossing the streets, stubbornly head-butting anyone in their way, and Sunday swims at the beaches, a tradition among Jamaican men and their families. *Yeah, life was different then. So much I went through to get to this point,* he thought as he flashed through memories of his youth.

CHAPTER 6

MS. BELINDA

As a child, Lemar was intelligent, overly curious, and an energetic four-year-old Caribbean Jamaican boy entering childcare for the very first time. This was an uncertain time for Lemar and his parents. While his parents, Viola and Earl, were separated, they maintained an amicable relationship as they co-parented. They each had their own apartment-flats between which Lemar split his time, primarily with his mother.

Initially, Viola stayed at home with Lemar while she focused on settling into her new apartment flat. She did odd jobs to make ends meet. As a single parent, Viola now had to figure things out the best way she could. It was hard for her to meet the everyday household expenses and pay for childcare, so she often had to leave Lemar home while she ran out for groceries. She'd usually ask her next-door neighbors to keep an eye out for him while she was away.

As most parents do, Viola wanted to shield Lemar from her struggles, as she intended to ensure his happiness. However, the need for cash flow became increasingly dire, so she returned to work and hired someone to look after Lemar.

Lemar rarely voluntarily woke up before eight o'clock in the morning. This day was no exception, except that it was his mother's first day back at work and the day he would meet his new babysitter. When Lemar awoke from his slumber, he peeped at an older, unfamiliar woman walking past his bed, set up in the corner of their living room. Lemar greeted the stranger. "Good morning."

She replied, "Good morning Lemar. My name is Miss Belinda. Are you ready for some breakfast?"

Lemar respectfully said, "Yes. Thank you."

Lemar sat at the table to eat his breakfast, a thick slice of toasted hard-dough bread with a pad of butter melting on top and a cup of fresh mint tea. After praying over his food, he was startled by the harsh sound of Miss Belinda's voice. "By the way, little boy, I don't play around with little children!" Lemar looked up at her as he listened. Her words were strange, but even stranger was what he saw her doing. She dangled and waved a brown leather belt in one hand and the other pointed in his direction. Once she concluded her threat, she rested the strap on top of the highest kitchen cabinet to keep it visible but out of his reach. Her scare tactic frightened Lemar as she intended. *This is only my first day with this lady, and already she's threatening me with a leather belt!* Lemar thought to himself, making sure not to appear defiant to his babysitter.

The rest of the morning was uneventful. Lemar walked gently on eggshells so as not to upset Miss Belinda. He asked for permission before going into the backyard through the kitchen back door. While playing outside next to a cage of pigeons and stirring up dust, his clothes got a little dirty. Miss Belinda warned him, "Stop getting your clothes so dirty little boy! I have to wash your clothes!" Lemar didn't like being called "little boy," and he cringed each time she referred to him as such. She only called him by his name once, and it's been "little boy" ever since. He pouted and thought, *this old grump!* As soon as she turned her back.

Miss Belinda called, "Come and have your lunch!" At the thought of having lunch Lemar forgot about his fear of her and ran to eat. She cooked a can of sardines, bread, and lemonade. She poured his beverage into a small drinking glass instead of his plastic cup in front of his seat. Lemar settled into the chair and proceeded to enjoy his lunch. There was also a fly buzzing around as Lemar ate. He always hated flies. *They're so dirty; they always land on garbage and stuff. Nasty!!*

The fly swooped past his food, perhaps to measure where it would land. He watched the fly like a predator stalking its prey. The fly landed on the placemat between his plate and the drinking glass. Lemar had already channeled his favorite cartoon character, Hong Kong Fuey, and postured his right hand to make a fatal strike at this fly. "HAIEEE-YAI!" he yelled as he brought his hand down on the table with a swift karate chop. He struck the fly with this fatal blow, leaving it dead on the table. His eyes opened wide in amazement. *My first fly kill!* He excitedly thought to himself. *Hong Kong Fuey was right! My karate chop worked!*

Miss Belinda was in the kitchen at the sink and saw everything. Lemar looked up at her, thinking she would be just as proud and ready to praise him. But she had another focus; the drinking glass was knocked forward during Lemar's fly attack. It crashed into the glass salt and pepper shakers, lemonade spilled, and a large piece of the drinking glass was chipped off at the top. Lemar's expectation of praise soon turned to fear as Miss Belinda reached up onto the kitchen cabinet and took down the belt. She lashed the whip, landing three good swipes. He was shocked as his face melted into tears. He looked at her with his red, teary eyes thinking, *she hit me with the belt, and I don't even know her.* Though struck with fear, he was smart enough not to open his mouth and speak.

Miss Belinda cleaned the table and the broken glass and discarded the dead fly. She then gave him water in his plastic cup and urged him to finish his lunch. *She should have given me my plastic cup, to begin with, and I wouldn't have broken the glass*, thought Lemar as he forced down the rest of his lunch.

After lunch, Miss Belinda sent Lemar for a nap. When he awoke from his slumber, she set his bath, watched him playfully and painfully wash himself, then helped him put on clean, fresh clothes. Lemar played for a while, careful not to break anything or cause a disturbance. He quietly ate his dinner and kept his placemat nice and neat. If he spied any flies, he planned to leave them in peace. Lemar did not want to upset Miss Belinda and feel her wrath again.

Viola arrived home from work, and Lemar was thrilled to see his mother, "Mommeee!" As Miss Belinda prepared herself to leave for the day, changing from her frumpy work duds into nicer clothing. She walked towards the front door, turned to Lemar, smirked, and said, "Good evening. I will see you tomorrow!" Her voice was almost sinister, sending chills up Lemar's spine. Lemar replied softly, "Good evening." He still felt the sting from the welts he had received earlier.

Lemar lifted his shirt and looked at the welts on his skin. He was still confused about the spanking. He didn't want to alarm his mother, so he crept into bed to hide his physical and emotional trauma. He was already dreading the day ahead. When Viola kissed him good night, he pretended to be already asleep. She assumed he was tired; she had no clue how afraid he was.

The following day, Lemar woke up late and found Miss Belinda in the kitchen. She gave him a snarl. The look on her face communicated the unspoken words, "Go ahead and make your next mistake!" On this day, Lemar managed to walk gingerly. He barely played outside. He kept his clothes clean and followed Miss Belinda's instructions like a soldier in the army. Lemar stayed near his bed most of the day, quietly nursing his wounds. He figured he'd be safe from Miss Belinda's wrath if he stayed in his haven. When Viola arrived home that evening, Lemar hugged her lightly and went to bed early, keeping his painful secret tucked away.

Wednesday morning came, and so did Miss Belinda. Lemar did well tiptoeing around Miss Belinda. But then he got complacent and let his guard down. After getting permission from Miss Belinda to play in the backyard again, he accidentally got his shirt dirty. Lemar ran inside to show Miss Belinda, thinking his honesty would earn him favor with her. Unfortunately, he was met with discipline instead of praise. She got her belt down and gave him a lashing.

Sleep became Lemar's best friend, and it kept him away from anything that could get him into trouble. He skipped lunch as he went to sleep just before lunchtime. He stayed in his bed throughout the afternoon. He did all he could to keep out of the path of Miss Belinda. She instructed him to bathe again late in the afternoon before giving him dinner. As he ate dinner, he thought, *she must have bad kids at home to be so mean to me*. She bid him farewell as she departed that evening, "Good evening. See you tomorrow." Lemar replied, "Good evening."

Viola's minibus driver kept getting stuck in rush-hour traffic, so she was late getting home. Miss Belinda seeing the time, decided to inform the neighbor, Ms. Sherry, to look in on Lemar as she left for the evening. As Ms. Sherry peeped in the front door, she saw Lemar sitting in the living room on his bed. Lemar said, "good evening Ms. Sherry."

"Good evening Lemar. I'm just checking on you. Are you okay?"

Lemar briefly looks out the front door at Ms. Belinda exiting the yard through the front gate. Afraid to tell, he says to Ms.

Sherry, "I'm fine, thank you."

Ms. Sherry closes the front door behind herself. Lemar stays up after she leaves, staring again at the welts on his waist by lifting his newly adorned clean shirt. He contemplated telling his mother what was going on. *I can't take it again. This lady's been here three days, and she's beating me! I don't like her! I'M GOING TO TELL MY MOMMY!* Instead of being greeted by a happy Lemar, Viola found Lemar sitting up with red eyes and tears streaming down his cheeks. She sprang into action, hugging and consoling her son.

"What's wrong, baby?" she asked concerned.

"MOMMY! That lady's been beating me with a belt! I'm scared of her. I can't take it anymore!"

Shocked, Viola inquired, "What belt?"

Lemar continued through his tears, "She beat me with a brown belt, and she put it on top of the big cabinet in the kitchen."

"Look, mommy," Lemar grimaced as he lifted his shirt over his welts and lowered the waistline of his pants to show her the marks on his skin from the beatings.

Viola was stunned by the sight of his bruises, and she maintained her composure while Lemar uttered his story. He grabbed his mother by the hand and led her down the hallway and into the kitchen. He pointed to the top of the cabinet above the sink,

Miss Belinda's hideaway. Viola followed Lemar's navigation, stretched to reach toward the back of the cabinet, and immediately pulled down the brown leather belt hidden there. She looked at Lemar's skin, then at the belt, and stared upwards briefly. Her heart sank, and rage flowed in.

Overcome with disbelief. Viola felt wrought with guilt and full of rage. Viola composed herself, looked at Lemar, and assured him, "Don't worry, Lemar, she won't be coming back here anymore. I'm taking you to stay with your father tonight. I'll deal with Miss Belinda in the morning!"

The next evening, Earl drove Lemar back to Viola's apartment. He was relieved to know Viola was letting go of Miss Belinda. Viola greeted Lemar with a big hug and kiss, then told him, "Go inside. Everything is fine, baby. I need to speak with your dad."

Lemar replied, "Okay, mommy. Bye, daddy."

"Bye-bye Lem, be good and behave yourself."

Lemar answered happily, "Okay, daddy!" and ran inside the apartment.

As Lemar surveyed the apartment, he kept an eye for any signs of Miss Belinda. He spotted the brown leather belt sitting on the kitchen table. He froze in fear, afraid to move a limb. But then he remembered, mommy said, "Everything is fine." Lemar began to calm down. His eyes scoured the apartment-flat one more time, and then he let out a sigh of relief. Viola entered and walked past Lemar, who was now sitting on his bed. She went straight into the kitchen and retrieved the belt. She came back into the living room and sat down next to Lemar. "Don't worry, baby. Miss Belinda won't be coming back here anymore. I'm cutting up this belt, and You'll never have to be reminded of her again." Viola reassured her son.

Viola took a pair of seamstress scissors, held one end of the belt, and told Lemar to hold the other. As she struggled to cut through the leather, she and Lemar felt a sense of relief. The past was being cut away, and they were looking toward a safer future. Viola threw the strap end of the belt into the garbage and kept the end with the buckle. She used it to tie up and mend her favorite broken-flower pot wrapped with burlap, which housed her favorite hibiscus plant. "This belt is good for dirt!" Viola declared.

Lemar was relieved and replied, "Yes, mommy, thank you, mommy!" The villain was gone. Viola and Lemar slept peacefully that night.

CHAPTER 7

FOR RICHER

FOR POORER

After losing some of her property Brownie feared that her bad choices would become like a generational curse. Brownie hoped that none of her children would experience the betrayal she once had. She hoped that the chains of naivety would be broken when she transferred ownership of her house to her daughter Celine. Brownie believed her former friend Eva was the last "real vampire" to attack her family. She didn't anticipate that Celine was ripe for her own demons to attack.

Ms. Dafne, the mother of Celine's last husband, Mr. Milton, persuaded Celine to add his name to the property title for the land she inherited from her mother. Dafne cunningly manipulates Celine's love for her son Milton and appeals to Celine's emotions, "You're both not getting any younger, and he's not going anywhere."

Celine made the same mistake as her mother, but this time she was duped in her decision with her eyes wide open. Perceived love and affection from her last husband and his mother exposed Celine's vulnerabilities and opened her up to deceit. Her frustration with the pain she encountered from being taken advantage of stirred up her salty satire and fiery attitude, but would she protect her daughters from the users she and Brownie had faced?

Brownie was often frustrated with Celine's poor decisions and choices in men. Although Celine worked hard for the sake of her children, Brownie wished she would push for higher goals for herself. Brownie often said to her, "Look at the 'Who-You-Bird'!

Just can't seem to take off and fly."

Meshel, the most outspoken, would be first to ask, "Grandma Brownie, what's a 'Who-You-Bird'?" Brownie would then simply answer, "that's a bird that just can't seem to take flight." Brownie's criticism often hurt Celine's feelings. Celine would sometimes laugh at the insult, and other times she'd snap back at her mother, "stop talking, your foolishness!"

Celine silently agreed with her mother. She knew that with so many children to feed, she pretty much dug herself into a space hard to navigate and hard to escape. Her sense of responsibility for her children was strong yet strange. She ran a strict schedule at home, feeding them their meals every day like clockwork. However, her loyalty to her children was questionable with the presence of each new man in her life.

The children she raised, Estelle, Roger, Meshel, Pamela, and Roland, all felt that their life was like competing to gain their mother's loyalty. As Celine's new love interests appeared, her loyalty seemed to sway away from the children of her previous relationships. Perhaps her children reminded her too much of their fathers, with each relationship's disappointments and pain.

A few of her other children were permanently raised by friends, and she occasionally sent Estelle and Roger to be cared for by other family members. There were numerous requests and pleas from older family members to have one of her children for themselves to raise. Celine wanted more for her children and knew she wasn't in any position to give them a better life. Her love for them provoked her to find homes where they'd be cared for.

As she was going through the divorce from her first husband, Celine needed to return home to live with her mother, Brownie, and younger brother Greg. Celine immediately realized that Brownie hadn't been keeping up with the bills upon returning home. Her tax and utility bills were outstanding, and the house was in danger of being taken by the government. Brownie's "Who-You-Bird" wasn't ready to take on the burden of resolving her mother's financial issues. But despite her inclination to take the wrong flight, she realized Brownie's problems would soon become hers.

CHAPTER 8

MY SISTER

MY FRIEND

Meshel's best friend for life was her younger sister, Pamela. She could always rely on Pamela to listen to her whenever she was upset. Pamela and Meshel may not have agreed or shared the same perspectives on everything, but Pamela always made time to listen to her older sister. They were one year apart, and both shared the 'middle-child syndrome.' Neither was praised like their older brothers and sisters, often ignored, and certainly not pampered like their youngest siblings. Perhaps one of the most crucial bonds was their commonplace among their siblings.

Meshel and Pamela had different personalities; however, they shared similar tastes in clothes, partying, and boys. These commonalities secured their bond. Their differing perspectives about their mother, Celine, were also sticking points in their relationship.

Pamela was more supportive of Celine than Meshel, regardless of how her mother's poor decisions affected her. She sympathized with her mother, "Mammi is doing her best!" Pamela would jump to her defense. Meshel, on the other hand, wasn't as empathetic. She resented Celine for not making her children her number one priority, and she hated that her mother decided to put a new man, Mr. Milton, ahead of them. But, regardless of their opposing views on compassion for their mother, Meshel and Pamela were thick-as-thieves. If you bothered one, you bothered both. They constantly watched each other's backs!

CHAPTER 9

SAINT VITUS DANCE

Lemar's right eye often blinked in multiple rapid spurts. Older folks in his neighborhood erroneously referred to it as the "Saint Vitus Dance." Saint Vitus Dance was a streptococcal disorder, and they presumed this was the cause of his ailment. However, the rapid spurts of blinking were caused by an unfortunate playground accident when he was five years old in the first grade.

It was another typical day at school as Lemar and his classmates played outside during lunchtime.

"Let's play tag in the yard!" yelled Floyd, the school miscreant and one of Lemar's classmates.

As the boys began to play, one of the lunch monitors reminded them, "Do not go outside the school gates!"

The school gates had recently been changed. Tall, aluminum tubular framed, chain-link gate panels replaced the eight-foot-high, wrought iron rusty dungeon bars. The old iron gates were left inside the school, awaiting disposal. Each gate was set standing upright, leaning against unpainted cinder block walls. The concrete walls had small circular openings spread about eight feet apart. The spaces were low and large enough for a child to fit their arm through easily.

Lemar's classmate, Floyd, intended to break the school's rules and go outside the gate. However, he knew 'goody-two-shoe' Lemar would never break the rules. So, he decided to try and lure Lemar beyond the gates by declaring, "outside of the gate is the safe zone," thinking, *if Lemar wants to try and tag me, he has to come outside of the gate to chase me back in!*

"You can't catch me!" Floyd teased Lemar.

Lemar chased Floyd to the gate but wouldn't follow him out. *I was right! He's too much of a chicken to come outside the gates,* thought Floyd to himself.

Floyd ran over to the concrete wall and stuck his hand through one of the open holes. Lemar saw the wiggling hand on his side of the wall and immediately walked over to it. Floyd quickly pulled his hand back and began randomly sticking his hand through each of the open holes. Lemar laughed and tried to anticipate which hole Floyd's hand would come through next. By the third try, Lemar guessed correctly. He saw Floyd's hand reaching through the hole. Both boys laughed at the fun they were having, but Floyd had something more sinister in mind. This time, instead of sticking his hand through the hole and pulling it back, Floyd put his hand through, grabbed hold of one of the old iron gates, and pushed it toward Lemar. Before Lemar knew it, the iron gate toppled, then began to plummet toward his head. Lemar instantly used both hands to guard himself against the gate as it descended on him. The gate proved too heavy for him, pinning him to the ground while one of the iron spikes at the top pierced his face next to his left eye.

Lemar's little body lay pinned under the gate screaming, "Mommy! Mommy! Mommy!" One of the older boys, Julius, saw what had happened and was strong enough to lift the gate off Lemar. Julius then picked up the much smaller Lemar, scurrying him to the school nurse's office.

Lemar's blood-soaked shirt brought nurse Joanne into action, as she immediately instructed Julius to put Lemar on her table. Breathless from his efforts, Julius gave nurse Joanne an account of what he saw happen to Lemar at the hands of Floyd. Nurse Joanne settled Lemar on her examination table and immediately performed triage to determine the extent of the damage to Lemar. She dabbed the blood off his face, neck, and chest, but the bleeding was too much to stop immediately.

Lemar lay still on his back as Nurse Joanne continued to dab the blood away from his face. She opened his shirt and examined him further, checking for any injuries to his chest or neck. There were none, so she closed his unbuttoned shirt like drapes across his chest to keep him warm. The piercing was so close to the corner of his eye that it was hard to tell where the cut ended. She thought to herself as she dared not say it for fear of Lemar's panic. *This child could have been pierced in the eye by this spike. It's a miracle he didn't lose his eye. I pray he doesn't lose his vision.*

Floyd was laughing crazily at first as the gate fell on Lemar, and then he tried to run away.

Another school monitor had also seen the incident from afar and shouted at Floyd. "You boy! Come here!!"

Of course, Floyd's little legs were not fast enough to escape. The stronger-faster monitor apprehended him, cuffed him with tight grips around his neck and arm, and brought the little scoundrel to nurse Joanne's office. Floyd was then forced to sit still in a chair outside the nurse's door as he watched Nurse Joanne treat Lemar's bloody wounds.

At first, Lemar was clearly in shock, lying silently in the room, not even crying. As soon as he saw the cotton gauze soaked in his blood, his shock withdrew, and he cried out of fear. Nurse Joanne was amazed at how quiet he was at first, but now Lemar was vocal, his desire uttered with intense screams, "MOMMY! MOMMY! I WANT MY MOMMY!"

"Relax, sweetheart," nurse Joanne said, interrupting his screams to reassure him with a calm, motherly voice. "You don't have to go back to class. Your father was called, and he's coming to pick you up."

Lemar calmed down and refocused his mind on the comfort and anticipation of his dad Earl's arrival. He tried his best to relax, looking out a window above his head and into the sunlit sky. He looked as he cried himself softly to sleep.

While he slept, nurse Joanne scolded Floyd. "You little wretch! What were you thinking? He could lose his eye. Why would you do such a vicious thing to him? I'm going to make sure the principal sees this so he can deal with you!" Floyd's heart sank in his chest, fearing his punishments but not regretting his actions. Back and forth, his face went from smirks-to-frowns. Clearly, he was a disturbed little boy.

The principal came to the nurse's office to see Lemar, but Lemar was already asleep. He scathed Floyd and gave him a severe tongue lashing and his final notice. "This is the last time you will hurt one of these children in this school!" The principal took Floyd by the arm to his office for further disciplinary action. Nurse Joanne asked that Lemar's father be told to bring a clean shirt so she could change him out of the bloody shirt. After examining the evidence for himself, the principal had made the phone call to Earl and was chomping-at-the-bit to see Floyd's parents. For all the times they offered excuses for their son Floyd's behavior, this evidence was the final straw and the final meeting. Floyd was immediately expelled from school. No more excuses!

At the sound of Earl's voice, Lemar awoke. "Hey, son." His eyes opened, focusing directly into the eyes of his dad Earl who stood above looking back at him on the table. Earl was relieved as his son looked up at him but soon revealed his anger as he visually scanned Lemar's injuries and blood-soaked clothing. Earl sucked his own teeth in anger through clenched lips, giving even nurse Joanne a bit of a scare.

Lemar was taken straight to the hospital near New Kingston to see a doctor. The resident staff doctor, Dr. Marsh, lifted the cotton gauze to find out the extent of the injury. Dr. Marsh even winced, looking at Lemar's severe wound like it was his own child's injury. He regained composure, looked up at Earl, and said chokingly, "Uhm . . . He needs stitches, sir!"

"Daddy! What are stitches?" Lemar inquired, looking for eye contact with Earl to gauge his response.

Slightly nervous and not wanting to cause Lemar to panic, Earl looked away, then looked back at Lemar. Feeling pressured, he released a sigh and answered calmly, "Lem, the doctor has to use a needle and special thread to sew your skin back together."

"Will it hurt?" Lemar asked, still looking for eye contact, still gauging safety through the reflection in his father's eyes.

"It shouldn't be too bad. Just a little bit at first." Earl confirmed.

Lemar knew what needle and thread meant. He saw his mother use them many times to hem his pants, sew buttons and sew clothing. "Oh! I've seen mommy use a needle and thread." He spoke.

"Something like that." Earl acknowledged.

Lemar looked at the curved needle as the doctor explained how he would stitch the wound. He thought, *why is the needle bent?* He didn't recall the needles his mother and aunt used being curved. "Doctor, I think that needle is broken," Lemar called out.

Earl and Dr. Marsh chuckled. "No. It's not broken, Lemar. It's curved so that it's easier to sew in the stitches," Dr. Marsh explained. "Now, I need you to sit very still while I get you all fixed up. By the way, you are a very brave boy."

Lemar smiled and sat up straight and as still as he could. He felt glad being called brave. Although he was still in pain, he wanted to show the doctor that he could handle the pain. Lemar grabbed his father's hand while the doctor first numbed the area around his eye, then put in the stitches.

Dr. Marsh cleaned up Lemar's wound, examined the stitches, and placed a big bandage on the side of his eye. "All done here. Thank you for sitting still, Lemar," the doctor smiled and turned to Earl. "He should have them in for a couple weeks. Then he'll come back to have them removed. I'm afraid to let you know that he may have a permanent scar, also, I can't say with certainty, but he may have some impact on the function of his eye or eye lid in time. We'll keep a close watch on it."

Earl fumed at the thought of Lemar having a permanent scar next to his left eye and possibly other issues. He wanted to lash out but knew he had to be calm for his son. As time passed, Lemar experienced a lasting effect on his left eye; he developed rapid eye spurts—a rapidly blinking eye. Saint Vitus dance.

CHAPTER 10

A BROKEN HEART

Meshel loved her grandma Brownie, as she was her favorite relative next to her father, David. Brownie taught her grandchildren about the bible and God's love, and she taught them about the discipline it took to return God's love. Sitting in her favorite tan bamboo chair with a red Chaconia flower print cushion, she often repeated her favorite saying, "Charity begins at home and ends abroad!" Brownie wanted her grandchildren to grow up with good manners, values, and morals.

Meshel and her siblings often asked Brownie, "What do you mean by 'Charity begins at home and ends abroad'?" Brownie would enjoy a soft hearty laugh and respond, "I'm just telling you; charity begins at home and ends abroad." Never providing any clarity for them, Meshel internalized and memorized her grandmother's credo before she was ten years old and made it her own doctrine throughout her life.

Kindness was important to Brownie, and she spent a great deal of her time grooming Meshel to behave respectably. Brownie imparted her wisdom on Meshel and often spoke in her version of a parable. She would say to Meshel, usually referring to her as "Mammi daughter, "Come here, Mammi daughter. 'member, anytime you have a stranger coming into your home, you might not have food, but always offer them a glass of water."

Brownie would share half of her white plastic plates of food with her grandchildren or strangers if they were hungry and had nothing to eat. She never seemed too tired of doing these acts of kindness or sacrifices. She lived by example for Meshel and the rest of her grandchildren.

At the core of her desires for her grandchildren was that they would love God and one another. Brownie wanted her grandchildren to keep a close relationship and to always look out for one another. For her, the family was everything, which is why she kept a close eye on her grandchildren. She loved the time she spent with them, and imparting her wisdom gave her great comfort that someone was teaching them the way they should go. Meshel especially hung on to every word that Brownie spoke. She was an attentive student and willingly adopted her grandmother's philosophies on life.

Brownie wanted to protect her grandchildren from the pain and loss that life can wreak. She emphasized the importance of family and togetherness because they can be taken away at any time. Brownie knew all too well about losing her family. At fourteen, her son was lost after a freak accident on the soccer field during a local schoolyard pickup game.

Charles was her fourth child. He was accidentally kicked in the chest during the game by an older boy from the opposing team. That evening after soccer, he came home bent over in pain.

"Charles, what happened to you?" Brownie asked, concerned about her son.

"Oh Mama, I'm alright. I was just playing ball with the guys." He casually replied through his gritted teeth.

"You sure? I should take you to see the people down the road; they could pray over you!" Brownie offered.

"No, Mama, I'm alright," Charles brushed it off.

But Charles never got better. His condition worsened; he had severe chest pains and frequently vomited that night. Brownie was afraid for her child's life, and she insisted that he let her take him to the local Spiritualist Priestess for prayer and healing. Charles finally agreed, and he and Brownie went to the church for worship. Unfortunately, despite their loud cries for the "spirits" to heal him, Charles died right there on the table.

"Charles! Charles!" Brownie cried in anguish. She realized she had made a grave error in trusting his severe medical condition to religious rites and not also seeking a medical doctor. The autopsy showed an abscess near his heart which developed from the force of the kick to his chest. Brownie was heartbroken. Despite her faith, Brownie was torn, which would be the only time anyone saw or heard her cry.

Charles was buried by the coconut palm tree field next to the church soon after he died. Brownie did not cry at his funeral. She held tight to her son Herman who was a year younger than Charles. She couldn't fathom the idea of losing another child. A few years later, Brownie gave birth to Celine and then Greg. They, too, were sheltered in her protective nest.

Brownie repeatedly told her grandchildren this story while sitting on her bamboo chair. She used it to remind them to be safe, that life was short, and that they should cherish each other while they had a chance to. "I had another son but lost him at fourteen, and it was the worst pain I ever felt. So you all take care of one another, eh?"

CHAPTER 11

MAKE ME BETTER

Lemar was an only child and often felt lonely as he didn't have any siblings at home to play with. Fortunately for him, both his parents now had cars and were always willing to drive him to playdates and to visit his friends. Yet this didn't fill the gap for Lemar. He wanted a sibling. He often bothered Viola whenever he asked her the dreaded question, "Mommy, can I have a brother or sister?"

Viola always diverted, "Ask your father."

Although Lemar was young, he understood that his parents' separation interfered with his dream of a sister or brother--an in-home playmate. His next best option was his older cousin Royce. Although he was eight years Lemar's senior, Lemar was attached to Royce. Royce lived three hours away in the countryside with Lemar's grandparents and his beloved Aunt Delores, so getting together wasn't always easy.

For the better part of his younger years, Lemar learned to play alone. So as he grew older, he was somewhat comfortable with being alone. Being alone had its benefits. Lemar's creativity was harnessed, and he learned to find projects to delve into.

Lemar's parents separated when he was four years old, but he saw his father every day after school. Sometimes Earl would take a late lunch to pick him up from school. Lemar would spend his time sitting in the waiting area while his father finished his workday. Earl's coworkers would walk down and see "Little Earl" sitting in his school clothes, patiently waiting for his dad. "Hello, Little Earl!" they'd say. Lemar felt welcomed and special. Although he was bored with nothing to do most of the time, he kept himself busy by studying cars driving by the glass windows, and people walking by the glass doors. Earl would come by to check on Lemar from time to time. Lemar would be excited to see his father as he hoped it was time to break free. However, he'd be disappointed when Earl said, "Relax. I'm not ready to leave yet."

At last, Earl would come down with his briefcase, and Lemar jumped up, grabbed his school bag, and headed to the garage. "Time to go home to Mom!" Earl reminded Lemar. Although Lemar was always happy to see his mother, he was unhappy about his parents being separated. Lemar desperately felt they all belonged together, under the same roof. He didn't understand why they couldn't be together, but he certainly understood the pain he felt splitting his time between homes. So on occasion, he would exaggerate not feeling well just so his parents could both come to his aid, and the three of them would be together. Viola would stay at Earl's apartment overnight to be close to her son and attend to his healing. For these brief moments, Lemar felt like he had a family.

At the age of six, Lemar experienced the fear of his first PTA meeting. He sat in the car while both his parents met with his teacher. He was nervous and anxious and wondered what the teacher would tell his parents. He wasn't a particularly disobedient or problematic child; however, he occasionally broke a rule or two. But his time alone helped develop him into a studious, focused, and diligent student.

Lemar saw the silhouette of his parents as they emerged from the dark of the evening into the parking lot's security spotlight. As they got closer to his father's car, Lemar could see the joy on their faces. Viola was ecstatic and could barely contain her excitement. She opened the door and exclaimed, "The teacher said you're a star student!".

Lemar was elated and looked at his father for a nod of agreement. Instead, Earl smirked and added, "But she said you talk too much in class!"

Lemar hung his head in shame. Viola pulled him close, hugged him tightly, and gave him two kisses on the cheek. Feeling a bit redeemed, Lemar still felt like he had to please his father to be fully accomplished in school. This was the beginning of the near-silent learner in life. Lemar was determined to study hard, behave accordingly, and excel academically. He wanted to please his parents but desperately sought his fathers' approval. Young yet mature, Lemar's future was defined.

CHAPTER 12

TRAUMA

Meshel was five years old when her mother, Celine, took her to spend a day with her paternal grandparents. Celine usually left Meshel with Brownie, but this particular day she decided that David's parents needed to fill in as babysitters while she went to party. She trusted Meshel would be safe with her grandparents and went along her way.

Soon after their arrival, Meshel made her way to her grandparents' yard, comforted herself on the swing set, and sang as she swung back and forth.

> *"Seesaw mother-in-law*
> *Seesaw — Seesaw*
> *Seesaw father-in-law*
> *Seesaw — Seesaw"*

Later that day, Meshel's sixteen-year-old cousin Joy stopped by to visit their grandparents, although she had an ulterior motive. Joy loved her grandparents, but typical of irresponsible teenagers, she wasn't interested in spending time with them when she visited; she was more concerned with hanging out with her friends and messing around with a boy from their neighborhood, Mike.

Joy spent most of her time dreaming out loud about her "crush on Mike." She shared secrets with her sisters about her desire to share her first kiss with Mike. Joy knew her mother and grandparents would disapprove of her behavior, yet she was willing to do anything to enjoy her puppy love. The day she visited her grandparents, she was thrilled to find Meshel visiting as well. Joy found the perfect excuse to make her way down to Mike's yard. Meshel was "adorable," and Joy wanted to "show off her little cousin." So, she persuaded Meshel to join her on a stroll to visit Mike. Meshel knew this was wrong and their grandparents would disapprove, but Joy was very persuasive, and before she knew what happened, Meshel and Joy were hand-in-hand heading towards Mike's yard.

Mike and a few friends were hanging out by his fence when Meshel and Joy arrived. They were greeted with a huge smile and a warm welcome by Mike. He marveled over Meshel and how "adorable she was." Mike didn't have any siblings and always wanted a little sister or brother. He thanked Joy for letting him meet her little cousin. Joy was elated that her plan to gain his attention worked. She now had no further use for Meshel, so she sent her off to play alone in the yard as she made her way back to the fence to be next to Mike.

There wasn't much to do in the yard, and Meshel was soon bored looking at the butterflies fluttering around.

"Joy! I want to go back to Gramma's house!" Meshel demanded. "I want to play on the swing, and I don't have anything to play with."

Joy was agitated with Meshel because she didn't want to leave

Mike and his friends.

"We'll go back when I'm ready, Meshel!" Joy snapped. "Now go back in the yard and find something to do!" She ordered Meshel as she turned her attention back to Mike.

Meshel was not happy and decided to take matters into her own hands. *I'm going back to Grandma and Grandpa's house by myself! I don't have to wait on Joy, she and that stupid boy!!* She thought.

Joy nor the boys noticed Meshel as she walked out of the yard and headed down the street. Meshel passed one of the neighbor's houses when she saw their dog lingering in their yard. The dog slowly paced towards Meshel as if it were hunting prey. She didn't notice its tail pointing straight up and not wagging as it normally would when indicating friendliness. Meshel wasn't afraid of dogs, so she didn't avoid its path. Instead, she attempted to greet and pet the dog's head, ignoring its low warning growl. As she stuck out her hand to make contact, the dog immediately snapped its jaws at her. With quick reflexes, Meshel quickly pulled her hand back, avoiding its bite. She freaked out, jumped up, and ran straight into the street without looking for oncoming traffic, right in the path of an oncoming car from around the curve of the road. The dog didn't chase her; because it heard and sensed the noise of the car's engine coming around the corner.

It was too late when Meshel realized the car was coming. The driver wasn't speeding, but the curves in the road limited his visibility. Their paths collided, and Meshel's little body was thrust into the air. As she came down and hit the pavement, her body rebounded as if it hit a spring mattress, elevating her into the air before landing motionless on the pavement.

Mr. Scanty, a local family man, heard the disturbing thud at the front of his car and immediately saw a small body flying through the air. He slammed on his brakes, put his car in park, and jumped out in shock as he looked at the small limp, motionless body laid out in the street.

With both his hands on the sides of his head, he cried tears, and he was devastated and too distraught to speak.

A small group of people immediately gathered around her body, all looking for signs of life. Meshel's father, David, happened to be working in the area that day when someone familiar with his family yelled, "David! A car just hit your daughter!"

David ran to the accident scene and knelt over his daughter's motionless body. He rubbed her cheek and whispered, "Meshel? Daddy's here! Meshel?"

He looked for signs of life—chest movements, head or eye movements, movement of her fingers or toes. He put his face by her nose to feel if breath came out of her nostrils. To his surprise, there was a faint breath as she exhaled. David was hopeful and continued to whisper to his daughter.

"Meshel. Come on, baby. Come on, daddy's girl. Wake up. Meshel, wake up, pleease!"

She didn't respond initially, but then she began opening her eyes. Her eyelids were bloody from the stream flowing out of the gash on her forehead. Meshel recognized her father's face; her vision was a bit blurry, and that's when David began to cry. Meshel, at this time, shed no tears as she watched her father cry. Her facial expressions were frozen. She was still in shock.

"Daddy, am I going to die? Am I going to die, daddy?" Was all Meshel could murmur.

"Hush, child, you're not going to die." David tried to reassure her. He carefully lifted her body from the ground as others from the crowd hailed a taxi for him. They all knew a cab would be the fastest way to get Meshel to the hospital, and waiting for an ambulance to arrive would have taken too long!

David slipped into the back seat and was careful not to disturb her body too much. She moaned in pain but felt safe in her father's arms.

"Daddy, am I going to die?" Meshel asked again.

He fought back his tears, not sure if she would survive the wounds from her accident. David maintained eye contact with Meshel and tried to hold a smile on his face in an attempt to reassure her. He didn't want her to see his fear. He calmly repeated, "No child, you're not going to die."

"Drive faster! Please drive faster!" David urged the taxi driver.

At the hospital, the doctors updated David on Meshel's injuries. She had bruises on her head but no serious damage. However, her ankle was badly broken and would require major surgery.

Meshel spent three months in a wheelchair. Once she could get on her feet again, she spent another six months in physical therapy to help her walk properly. It was a little more than a year before she fully recovered.

Mr. Scanty, the driver, was detained at the accident scene. As the police finally arrived, they processed paperwork for the incident. Later the officers spoke with David and checked in on Meshel. Contrary to expectations, the officers had good words for David about Mr. Scanty - he was not charged with a crime.

Three days after the accident, Mr. Scanty found his way to the hospital to make amends. Finding Meshel and her parents, he offered his sincere apologies. He also offered Meshel lots of little packets of orange juice, grape juice, kiss-cakes, Twinkie-like pastries, and cheese doodles. "I am so sorry. I'm so sorry. Please forgive me?" He repeatedly begged Celine and David. I have been praying for her every day since the accident. "I have my own local grocery store; if you need anything for her or your family, just come to the store and ask, and I will provide it. I am so sorry." Mr. Scanty pleaded.

David, who would have loved to throw punches at Mr. Scanty, found himself surrendering his anger and instead consoled Mr. Scanty, who began to shed tears at the sight of Meshel in her hospital bed, her leg in a cast elevated high by a sling.

Meshel's recovery period brought about some peace between her parents. They were both so focused on her well-being that they remembered how to be amicable with one another. This was the best part of recovering for Meshel. She loved seeing her parents get along and be in the same room without an argument.

David and Celine fought all the time before Meshel's accident. They constantly argued over what was best for Meshel, Pamela, and Roland. David felt like Celine wasn't a responsible mother. Celine felt trapped trying to raise so many children while she worked, and she resented not having time for herself. He wasn't happy that she'd left Meshel with his elderly parents while partying with her friends. He blamed her for what happened to Meshel. However, they kept their bickering under wraps while nursing their little Meshel back to health. This was a time Meshel would hold dear in her heart for years to come, as it was one of the only times she witnessed her parents being kind to one another. During this time, Celine was also very kind to Meshel.

Unfortunately, Meshel's parents returned to their old bickering ways after she recovered. While her body was healed, her heart was still broken. The trauma from the car accident left Meshel with a lifelong fear of crossing the street. It also left her traumatized by the shattered hopes that her parents would rekindle their relationship once she could walk again.

CHAPTER 13

GRANDSON

Lemar blossomed academically at a young age. He passed his junior high school entrance exams at the age of nine. Earlier that year, he represented his prep school at the National Spelling Bee competition and placed fifteenth out of sixty-three kids. Lemar often recalled the word that ended his rise to the National Spelling Bee Championship, SOCIETY.

"S-O…S-I-E-T-Y."

"No. That is incorrect. Society. S-O-C…I-E-T-Y," the proctor, Mr. Andrews, spells out as he stresses the "C" in the correct spelling.

Lemar was disappointed, upset, and embarrassed, but he left the stage calmly and sat next to his chaperone, Miss Jones. "Don't worry Lemar, you did very well. You'll be even better next year." said Miss Jones. While Lemar could spell much more complex words, he stumbled and misspelled society based on its phonetic sound. The winner, Vincent, was thirteen years old. Vincent was able to spell "Erysipelas" seven different ways. Lemar was in awe and even heard adults in the room gasping, amazed at Vincent's answers. *How is that possible?* Lemar thought to himself.

Mr. Andrews smiled at Vincent, as he confirmed, "THAT IS CORRECT!" This encouraged Lemar to study harder for the following year's Spelling Bee, and he was now more determined to do even better academically.

"Dad, can I go to math class on Saturdays at school?" Lemar

asked, then continued, "The teacher said it's one dollar for each class, and I could become even better at Math."

Earl considered the cost and said, "Okay, Lem," his pet name for Lemar.

As a young man, Earl attended a religious high school. He was a solid academic and encouraged Lemar's desire to perform well in school. Strict school culture groomed Earl into the type of father he was to Lemar. He not only encouraged good grades, he demanded them along with discipline. Earl hardly ever used foul language in Lemar's presence, although most of his adult friends often used profanity.

Despite grandpa Franz's objections to the expensive school fees, Earl's mother, Marcy, insisted that Earl attend the school. "He has to get the education!" She fought back with her husband. While Marcy never attended school as a child, she wanted her children to graduate with an education. All except for Earl's youngest brother Vee, who would be held back from school to afford Earl's education. Earl agreed with his parents to help Vee after he completed school, but Vee never agreed to this deal; he felt cheated. Vee never let Earl live down his privilege of education at his expense, and he carried his resentment towards Earl well into their adult years.

Earl loved his mother more for insisting he got the education he needed to succeed, not only for himself but for their family. Sometimes families are faced with choices and sacrifices made out of love. However, some decisions can lead to resentment and disagreement and may even cause hatred among family members. The damage may be reversible through forgiveness, but in the case of Vee and Earl, reconciliation was way off on the horizon.

Lemar's grandmother, Grandma Marcy, loved him, and he loved her too. She often admitted that he was one of her favorite grandchildren, especially since he often visited her. Although his cousin Royce lived with her, Lemar held a special place in her heart. Lemar would occasionally stroll with her to the local store. He never complained about how slow they had to walk due to his grandmother's debilitated knocked knees, which eventually forced her to walk with a cane. Lemar never inquired about her disability, and later in life, he learned a more sensitive and loving way to refer to her debilitating illness; "loving knees."

Lemar and Grandma Marcy would slowly walk down a partially paved road to the elevated wooden shack, which operated as a grocery store. The steps were too much for her to handle as the advanced stages of arthritis in her knees riddled her with pain.

"Go in and give this list to the storekeeper!" She'd hand her shopping list to Lemar. "Here's the money. Make sure he [the shopkeeper] writes down the price of each item. And make sure you count the change after you pay." Grandma Marcy knew that Lemar was good at math and trusted that he could handle the financial exchange.

"Yes, Gramma," Lemar would reply as he jog-trotted off with her shopping list and a handful of cash. He didn't deviate from her instructions; he picked up each item on her list, handed the list to the shopkeeper, and asked that he write down the price of each item. Then Lemar tallied the cost with the storekeeper. He then paid for the items and accurately counted the change he received.

The time spent with his grandmother would be etched in Lemar's heart forever, and he carried those moments with him. Grandma Marcy looked forward to the quality time she and her Lemar spent together. She marveled at how smart he was, which made her incredibly overjoyed. She loved that she could trust him to be gentle, understanding, and trustworthy.

CHAPTER 14

FATHER

Although the men of the family, Earl, Grandpa Franz, Royce, and Uncle Vee, all enticed Lemar to be "strong like them." It would be the women of the family, Viola, Grandma Marcy, and his Aunt Delores, that would be first to teach him about the importance of God. They all took him to church as often as they attended, and his grandmother's philosophy was, "Speak the truth and speak it well, Amen!" While Grandma Marcy could not read or write, she always advocated for believing in God and getting an education. Viola deeply introduced Lemar to God when he was eight years old.

"Lemar!" she summoned him.

"Yes, mommy!" he obediently answered.

"I want to talk to you about God," Viola said.

"Okay, mommy," Lemar responded, curious about the talk.

Viola continued and instructed, "You are to love God more than you love me!"

"But mommy..." Lemar disagreed and tried to interject.

Viola overrode his interruption, "I'm telling you, son. You are to love God more than you love me!"

"But mommy, you cook for me and take care of me and...." Lemar tried to convince Viola.

"I know, son, but God gives me everything I do for you. You are always to love God more than you love mommy, okay?" Viola gently explained.

"O... oh...Okay, mommy." Lemar surrendered.

Lemar sat still, sad and confused. Viola walked away, leaving him behind on the porch to think about what she had said. As he sat in silence, the noise of the crickets seemed louder that night. Lemar never forgot his mother's words.

When Lemar turned thirteen, he had another memorable moment of the importance of believing in the bible and God. His Grandpa Franz sat and read the bible on the front porch of Earl's house several days a week, anywhere from a half-hour to one-hour. Grandpa Franz toted his Bible and his magnifying glass in one hand. After he finished his reading, Grandpa Franz would stand in front of the security bars by the porch, staring out at the hills far off in front of the house. Lemar would often sit and watch, wondering, what is he thinking about? Occasionally, Grandpa Franz would glance over his shoulder at Lemar. Lemar never disturbed him; instead, he just sat and quietly observed.

Grandpa Franz was a man of very few words, so when he decided to have a talk with Lemar about God, Lemar knew he needed to listen attentively. Lemar was sitting inside the living room while his grandpa was standing by the security bars on the porch.

With his back turned to the living-room, he called out in a firm breathy voice, "Lemar!"

"Yes, Grandpa," Lemar responded.

"Come here!" Grandpa Franz insisted.

Lemar walked to his grandfather and answered, "Yes, grandpa?"

"Son, you don't see me going to church as your grandmother does, but this bible here..." Grandpa Franz pointed to his bible on the front porch chair. He continued, "my son...it's in here! It is in here!"

Lemar looked over at the bible on the chair. Although his grandfather didn't say much, Lemar somehow understood that he was telling him that the bible is a book of trustworthy information.

"Always respect this book! It is in here!" Grandpa Franz commanded.

"Yes, grandpa," was all Lemar could say.

In that quick conversation, Lemar felt he was just given the compass to his direction in faith. At this stage of his life, he had no idea of the difficulties ahead; sheltered from a life of poverty, crime, and family drama. Lemar wasn't exempt from challenges, most of which seemed minor compared to those of his peers, but he dealt with them in solitary. In time he realized that his upbringing was a bit different from many of his friends and peers.

CHAPTER 15

FRIEND OR FOE

"Mammi!" Meshel called for her mother, Celine.

"Yes, Meshel," Celine answered, annoyed at the interruption.

"Can we go over to play with Adelle, pleeease?" Meshel pleaded. It was about 10 am.

Celine picked her head up and looked her daughter in the eye. "Cheese-on-bread! Meshel, you and Pamela don't like to stay in your own home? Why is it you all want to go to Adelle's home so much?"

Meshel had to think before she answered. "She has roller skates and a bicycle, and she lets us both use them."

"Alright, okay, you two go ahead, but take care not to break any of her things, eh! Lord knows I can't afford to pay back anyone if you break something, so be careful. Pleeaase be careful!" Celine urged. She felt a slight tinge of guilt that she couldn't give her children the things that made childhood more enjoyable. So, she didn't want to deny her girls the fun she couldn't afford. She also resented their father, David, because he couldn't help her with the finances needed to provide their daughters with anything more than the basics.

"Meshel, why did you lie to Mammi?" Pamela asked. "You know we only get to watch Adelle while she's roller skating, and she doesn't let us ride her bicycle at all!"

"Pamela, you're talking too loud; Mammi might hear you,"

Meshel whispered hurriedly. "She might, eventually?" Meshel hopefully added, "It won't happen if we don't try!" Meshel was bothered by Pamela's doubtful attitude.

Pamela was afraid that Meshel would get them into trouble because of her willingness to lie to their mother. She knew the risk of being punished was high if they were caught, not just because of the lie but also because of Celine's embarrassment. It was a typical sunny summer Bajan morning, already eighty-four degrees. Pamela and Meshel walked down the partially paved and rock-sprinkled road until they were in front of Adelle's home.

"Morning, Adelle!" Meshel called out. Adelle looked up from tying the laces on her skates and beckoned them to come into the yard with a wave of her hand.

"Morning Meshel, Morning Pamela," Adelle greeted them as they entered her yard. "Morning Adelle,' they replied in unison. "Come sit down over here! I have some new moves to show both of you!" Adelle exclaimed.

Meshel and Pamela took a seat on the steps near the driveway. Adelle started skating away from them and then turned around to skate backward. She then made the same move while skating back toward them.

"Wow, she can skate backward now?" Pamela said to Meshel as Adelle again skated away from them toward the front gate.

Meshel was moderately impressed and whispered to Pamela, "She should let us try to skate forward at least; she's so selfish!"

Meshel wanted to try skating, but she knew Adelle was not having any of that. She loved seeing Meshel and Pamela drool over her fancy toys. Meshel wasn't afraid to ask for anything she wanted. She was bold and didn't care if Pamela disagreed with her asking.

"Adelle, can we try a little bit of skating with your skates?" Meshel stood up and asked. Pamela was still sitting on the steps, quietly intrigued by Meshel's boldness. They both waited quietly for Adelle's answer.

"No, Meshel! My mother doesn't want me to lend my things to anybody, or I'll get in trouble." Adelle responded, rolling her eyes.

"But last week, when we walked by, we saw you lend your skates to your cousin!" Meshel snapped back, daring Adelle to challenge her.

Adelle froze for a moment, slightly afraid of Meshel and somewhat annoyed. "Uhm...Well, that's my cousin; she is family, so it's okay! I won't get into trouble for that!"

Meshel knew Adelle's mother was strict, but she wasn't convinced that Adelle didn't want to share with her and Pamela. Adelle took off her skates and placed them side-by-side on the porch at the top of the steps near the driveway. She then put on her flip-flop slippers and walked over to her bicycle. As she began riding, Meshel gave notice, "Okay, we're leaving now, we're going home, Adelle."

"You're leaving already?" Adelle asked.

"Yes, our big brother, Roger, said he was going to the store and would bring something back for us." Meshel lied, no longer wanting to be a spectator of Adelle enjoying her toys.

Adelle was curious, "Something like what?"

"We don't know," Pamela jumped in. At this point, she was equally annoyed with Adelle and joined in on Meshel's lie. "He's always surprising us. Last week he gave us bracelets, one each!" Pamela exclaimed.

"So, where are they?" asked Adelle, knowing their family didn't have the financial means for such things.

"We left them home! They're for going out and not for play-ing!" Meshel retorted. "We'll show it to you the next time we come over, as long as you let us use your skates and ride your bike!" Meshel attempted again to bargain, although her bargain-ing chip was fictitious.

Meshel and Pamela left to go home. "I wish we had things like Adelle," Pamela admitted.

"Yeah, her parents buy her so much toys to play with, and it's only for her! She doesn't have brothers or sisters to share with," Meshel added.

The two sisters held hands as they journeyed back home. It was almost midday as they walked into the house, and immediately they heard their oldest sister Estelle's voice.

"Meshel! Come here." Estelle summoned.

"Coming," Meshel called out. She sucked her teeth and thought, *what does she want with me now?*

"I'm going to the room," Pamela informed Meshel. She didn't want to be bothered with Estelle and knew the tone in her voice meant that drama was coming.

Because Celine had told her, Estelle knew that her sisters had just come from Adelle's house. Celine fell into another one of her moods, wishing she could do more for her children, and Estelle just happened to be close enough to hear her while she mused aloud about it.

"Meshel, do you realize Adelle never comes over to play with you and Pamela?" Estelle asked.

"Yes, Estelle, I know!" Meshel replied, annoyed by the question.

"Why do you think that is?" Estelle interrogated.

Meshel was stumped. She didn't quite understand why. She stood still and stared at Estelle.

"Meshel, Adelle doesn't come over here to play with you or allow you or Pamela to play with her toys because she thinks she's better than you and Pamela!" Estelle asserted.

Meshel pondered, she never let me, or Pamela wear her

skates, but she let her cousin wear them. She never lets us ride her bicycle, but she always wants us to watch her ride or push her uphill when needed. She always makes excuses as to why she can't come to our house, and she never allows us to go into her house. Finally, Meshel replied, "Estelle, yeah, you're right! She does think she's better than Pamela and me!" That was the last day that Meshel and Pamela visited Adelle.

After Estelle convinces Meshel to open her eyes to the real nature of her friendship with Adelle, she realizes her self-worth. Meshel was now determined to demand and expect respect from everyone, not just her family. She adopted a mantra and incorporated it as a daily reminder. I'm never going to take last place with anyone. It doesn't matter what they think I look like. I am somebody. Grandma Brownie always said to lift up my head! Meshel ingrained these positive reinforcements into her mind and heart, which would become her life's foundation.

Mammi wanted all her girls to understand the importance of knowing their self-worth. Being the second oldest of the bunch, seven years older than Meshel, Estelle was the first daughter to be taught. Her responsibility now was to pass on the lesson and reinforce those values with Meshel and Pamela. She had learned some hard lessons and was determined to ensure her little sisters were ready for what may come their way.

Meshel and Pamela were often referred to as "Irish twins." They were only a year apart in age. They often dressed alike and were inseparable. When one hurt, the other empathized. When one fought, the other was ready for battle. Although Meshel was one year older than Pamela, any life lesson she was taught was often applicable to Pamela. Throughout the years, Meshel often fought with Pamela to be her teacher, just as Estelle fought with Meshel to be hers.

CHAPTER 16

PEER PRESSURE

Lemar spent lunchtime with the other kids in the schoolyard playing in the sun as a youngster. They took cooling breaks under one of two big-sprawling Poinciana Trees before leaving the shade to re-engage in competition on the 'jungle gym' or 'monkey bars.' Boys would compete with boys doing somersaults on the bars. At times the girls would compete with the boys and each other, at the risk of exposing their undergarments or bloomers as their uniform skirts quickly turned upside down. After school, the children crowded by the main school gate, waiting to be picked up by parents or walking to the bus stop or home.

Lemar's parents, Earl and Viola, lived a short walk away from school, each in their own separate apartment flats. This was after their marriage separation. After school, Lemar was taught to walk home by himself to Earl's flat for homework and dinner. Earl hired a housekeeper, Ms. Claudia, to clean the house, cook, feed, and watch Lemar until her shift ended.

Lemar noticed one of his schoolmates, though not from his classroom, walking in the same direction. One day the young man approached Lemar to see if he'd be interested in walking home together after school. "Your name is Lemar, right?"

"Yes. Why?" Lemar asked, puzzled by how this boy had already learned his name.

"My name is Keith. I see you walk on the same road every day. You live around here?"

"Yes, I see you walking too. I walk to my father's house." Lemar answered.

"Alright." Keith reckoned, "you can walk with me after school then?" Almost demanding Lemar's company to walk together.

"Alright." Lemar agreed.

The deal was struck, so they began meeting at the school gate after school to walk home together. Keith lived further down the road than Lemar in the next neighborhood, and they initially always parted ways at the corner of Lemar's street. Then one day, Keith asked Lemar to walk with him further down the road.

"Lemar, can you walk down the road with me; just one more street?" Keith urged.

Lemar didn't think much about it and happily walked Keith to the next street before returning home. After a few days, Keith urged Lemar to walk with him even further.

"Why do you want me to walk further with you?" Lemar asked, fearing Keith's intentions.

"Oh, come on, it's just further down this road," Keith replied, irritated by the inquiry.

Lemar didn't feel entirely comfortable walking so far. But he did it just to please Keith and for the sake of the friendship. A few days later, Keith became brazen as he asked Lemar to walk further with him, this time onto a side-street. Again, Lemar obliged just to keep the friendship. The distance grew farther away from Lemar's home, and he had to run back to try and get home when the housekeeper, Ms. Claudia, expected him.

Ms. Claudia noticed that Lemar began arriving home a little later than usual. She raised an eyebrow but didn't ask any questions. Lemar didn't offer any excuses either. He would walk into the house, saying, "Afternoon, Ms. Claudia," and go straight to doing his homework.

By the third week of pushing the limits and getting home later-and-later, Ms. Claudia became agitated and curious about what was causing Lemar's tardiness, so she began clocking the time of his arrival. She hadn't decided to mention anything to Earl at the moment and wanted to gather facts first.

Thursday afternoon after school, Keith asked Lemar to walk him all the way home. This was way out of Lemar's comfort zone, and Keith was shocked to hear him refuse. "I'm not walking to your house! That's too far."

"You're a scaredy-cat! You're a chicken; come on!" Keith challenged Lemar.

"I'm not a scaredy-cat, but I'm not walking with you! I'm going to get in trouble if I get home late again. My father's housekeeper keeps looking at me weird every time I come home late from school," Lemar defended himself.

"If you don't walk with me to my house, I'm going to tell my father SHOOT YOU!" Keith threatened Lemar.

"What?" Lemar was stunned, frozen for a moment. He couldn't believe what his friend Keith had said to him.

"My father is a policeman; I'm going to tell him to shoot you!" Keith said, doubling down on his threat.

"Alright." Lemar agreed as he was too afraid to say no., *I can't believe Keith just threatened me. Or he's just joking or what?* Lemar wrestled between fear and his friendship, wondering how he got into this conundrum. But he couldn't shake the uneasy feeling floating in his belly.

Lemar arrived at his father's house nearly an hour later than his regular arrival time. Ms. Claudia was standing at the corner of his father's street, waiting for him. *Oh boy! Why is she out here?* Lemar thought to himself. *I'm in trouble now.*

"Where are you coming from?" She asked Lemar with a stern voice and a firm stare.

"From, From school...." He tried not to lie entirely and just omitted the walk between school and Keith's home.

"Boy, Don't lie to me! I've been watching you for the past three days! Who is that little boy you've been walking down the road with?" Ms. Claudia inquired. She surprised Lemar when she revealed that she'd been watching him, as he was sure his extended walks with Keith went unnoticed.

Lemar sighed; *time to let the truth out,* "That's my friend from school. His name is Keith. He asked me to walk home with him from school because we walk in the same direction. He kept asking me to walk further and further down the road; that's why I came home late. Sometimes I don't mind walking with him, and sometimes I worry my dad will find out. Today he asked me to walk him all the way home. I wasn't going to, and I said No. But then he told me his father is a policeman and he was going to tell his father to shoot me! I was afraid and decided to walk him most of the way home, and then I turned back. I don't know if his father would shoot me. I thought he was my friend…."

Ms. Claudia stood there, silent, while Lemar rambled on. Her irritation quickly turned to empathy towards Lemar. But her feelings toward Keith were quite the opposite. "Lemar, you don't fear that boy. His father can't shoot you. You're just a child, just like Keith. I will tell your father so he can straighten this out. You heard me? No more following Keith home! I'm going to tell your father about this! Alright? Let's go inside. Go do your homework."

"Ok, Ms. Claudia," Lemar replied. He was afraid of what his father might say and do, but he was also relieved at the same time. Strangely enough, he felt a burden lifted off his shoulders. He didn't like keeping things from his father.

The next day during lunchtime, Keith approached Lemar as if nothing had ever happened. "Lemar, you're walking me home today, right?"

Lemar didn't lift his head from his sandwich. He answered

Keith, "No. I'm not walking you home."

"So you're going to walk me halfway then, right?" Keith demanded.

Lemar looked up from his sandwich and replied, "No. I'm not walking you halfway. I got into trouble with my father."

Keith was shocked that Lemar pushed back and denied his demand. He stood there silently for a moment. Lemar sensed that Keith wasn't as tough as he pretended to be, so this boosted his courage.

Keith made one more desperate attempt, "I'm going to tell my father to SHOOT YOU if you don't walk with me to my house!"

Lemar paused. He remembered what Ms. Claudia told him and then shouted, "I'M NOT GOING TO WALK YOU HOME! AND YOUR FATHER IS NOT GOING TO SHOOT ME! HE'S PROBABLY GOING TO SPANK YOU FOR TELLING A LIE!"

From that day forward, Keith avoided Lemar. From time to time, they would see each other during lunchtime in school, but Keith would look back with a shameful look on his face every time. Perhaps he did get that spanking from his father. Maybe Earl did handle the situation but never told Lemar anything about it. Keith and Lemar occasionally saw each other as they still walked the same basic path after school, but they never exchanged words again.

CHAPTER 17

BULLY

While dressed in their school uniforms, Meshel and Pamela looked like most girls. Hair was neatly combed, white shoes, no makeup, clear nail polish or none at all, no large earrings or jewelry permitted, only small stud earrings and certainly no deviations from the dress code. Because of their ages, Meshel was one year ahead of Pamela in school, but they attended the same school and always met during lunchtime.

Pamela could handle herself if she had to fight, and she did when pushed to the limit. She often jumped on the backs of her brothers to play fight, never backing down from her brothers that loved their sisters dearly. They were rough, but they held back on her. Meshel never liked to play fight, as she feared she would get too angry, and it would go too far. At lunchtime, Meshel and Pamela would meet in the school cafeteria, or Meshel would go to Pamela's homeroom class.

One day, Meshel's teacher let her students leave one minute early for lunch, so Meshel decided that she would rush to meet Pamela in her homeroom instead of the cafeteria. As she walked down the covered pathway to Pamela's classroom building, she heard the tweeting sounds of 'sparky,' one of many Bajan bullfinch birds perched on the branch of a mango tree near the schoolyard. The sunshine felt good on her arms and face as she arrived at her destination. Most of Pamela's classmates were already out of the classroom for lunch, and Pamela was already gone. *Cheese-on-bread*, she thought. *Pamela's gone already?*

Meshel turned around and made her way toward the cafeteria. It was lunchtime, and many small groups of students were gathered in the schoolyard, making the most of their free time at lunch. There was a small skirmish, and Meshel caught it from the corner of her eyes. *Is that Pamela?* She thought. *Why is that girl in her face like that? What's going on?* In her panic, Meshel crushed her sandwich in her hand as she ran over to aid Pamela.

Pamela was unusually timid and had her face turned away from her aggressor. "What are you doing?" Meshel said. "That's my sister you're bothering!"

The other girl, Asharia, menaced Pamela and, seeing that Meshel was a little bigger than herself, replied, "Well, I'll call my big sister on you!"

"Call your sister if you want to. I'll beat her up, and I'll beat you up too!" Meshel responded.

Asharia ran off to get her big sister, a school student. Once Asharia's big sister Rhonda arrived, Rhonda recognized Meshel from her homeroom and respected Meshel's wit from some of the run-ins Meshel had with their teachers. The animosity was squashed immediately! Meshel now had a new friend in Rhonda. Rhonda respected Meshel's moxie and bravery in her speech. Rhonda and Meshel became inseparable. Besides Pamela, Rhonda was the only friend Meshel would hang out with.

It wasn't long before Rhonda's abusive behavior surfaced. Most of the girls in the neighborhood attended the same school, including a girl named Beverly.

Beverly's school uniform never seemed to be properly cleaned, her facial skin was always dry, and some students even said that she had lice in her hair. Beverly lived in abject poverty, and she slept on the bare floor of her mother's home at night.

One day at school, Rhonda said to Meshel, "let's beat up Beverly!" Meshel agreed to beat her up that day after school. They both cornered Beverly behind the same mango tree where the 'sparky' usually tweeted, having its choice of fallen mangoes burst open laying on the ground.

At first, Pamela had agreed to be part of the plan but then decided to back out before the end of school. Pamela was afraid of what Mammi would do if she found out she was bullying someone else. Guilt started to press on Meshel's conscience after Pamela backed out, but she still ran to do the wicked act with Rhonda.

Meshel pulled Beverly's hair as Rhonda kicked her a few times. Beverly covered her face, and she coiled her body into a tight knot to protect her vital organs. It wasn't the first time Beverly had undergone such an attack, and she barely had a scratch after they were done. They tried to embarrass her, humiliate her, and bully her into better hygiene, but it never occurred to them that talking to Beverly was a better option.

Little did they realize that afterward, Beverly would try to find both their homes with her uncle! "Is that the little girl who beat you up?"

"Yes, uncle," Beverly confirmed.

"Little girl, I want to speak to your parents."

Meshel knew right away that time was on her side, "they're not home and won't be home anytime soon!"

"Cheese-on-bread," Beverly's uncle said, fuming, "Alright, I'll wait!" and then he waited for about two hours. Finally, he gave up when it got dark for the evening, noisy crickets announcing themselves and other sinister sounds from the creatures of the night.

Meshel sighed in relief; Beverly's uncle left to find Rhonda's home. Almost every home in Rhonda's neighborhood looked alike, especially at night, so he couldn't find where she lived. Nobody told where anybody lived, to outsiders.

The next day at school, Meshel saw Rhonda. "Rhonda! Beverly and her uncle came to my house yesterday and asked to speak to my parents?"

Rhonda shocked Meshel with her response, "I heard they came to my community too, but they couldn't find my house. I want to go and beat her up again?"

Meshel thought, *Again!* Then she replied, "Nope! Not me. I'm not doing that anymore."

"Well, I don't care," replied Rhonda defiantly, "I'm going to beat her up again."

From that day forward, Meshel kept her distance from Rhonda. They were still classmates, so Meshel kept it casual, saying a simple "Hi" whenever she saw Rhonda at school or in their community.

To get back at Meshel and Rhonda, Beverly's uncle repeatedly told the community what they had done to his niece. "Rhonda and Meshel are not nice at all! They beat up my niece, and they cornered her by a mango tree, held on to her hair, and punched her up. Just because they think they're better than her."

Meshel tried her best to ward off her bad reputation by sticking to good behavior and faking her innocence of the accusation. "I Don't know why he's saying that," she repeatedly replied to Mammi's inquiries about the incident.

For the first time, Meshel had a taste of feeling like a 'villain' in her community. She didn't enjoy it, and she knew she was actually guilty!

CHAPTER 18

THE TOMBOY

Lemar had already learned some valuable life lessons at a young age. Viola often referred to him as her little 'old man' because Lemar often acted older than his age. While Viola was more vocal in teaching her son lessons about life, Earl seldom spoke about anything in life except to criticize the wrongdoings of others.

"These people don't know how to behave themselves." He would often say to Lemar.

When it came to the issue of fighting, Viola would often remind Lemar, "You Don't start any fight, but Don't let anyone punch you in your face! You hear me?"

Lemar understood that meant he should only fight to protect himself and for no other reason.

Whenever Lemar asked, "Daddy, what should I do if somebody wants to fight me?"

Earl responded, "Lem, I Don't like that 'fighting thing.' That's how people get hurt."

"But, daddy, what if somebody forces me to fight?"

Earl's customary final response, "Son, that's just how it goes."

Lemar was left to fill in the blanks on his own. He would not teach Lemar the art of fighting if he knew the art himself. Ironically, Earl was in tremendous shape! Lemar knew this as he often watched his dad exercise at the track and at home, but he never saw Earl in direct conflict with others.

Lemar managed well to handle himself with the boys, but he would soon face dealing with the girls. Viola often said, "Girls will only bother you when they like you. You better be careful because girls move like cats, and they may challenge, charm, or manipulate you to get their way."

Lemar learned to fight by rough housing with the boys at school—the way most boys earned their stripes. He didn't pick fights with others, but Lemar never backed down from a fight, except once.

One day while on the playground, Lemar was approached by a girl named Meryl Fessit. Meryl had a reputation as a brawler. She'd fought and won all the fights with the girls at school. Meryl was what most of the parents would call a "tomboy." She didn't mind getting dirty, playing with the boys, climbing, running, and fighting. While most of the other girls at school cared more about their uniforms, hair clips, and school shoes, by mid-day, Meryl's uniform often looked wrinkled and dirty, her hair disheveled, and her shoes dusty. She cornered Lemar at the end of lunchtime and challenged him to a fight. Lemar was caught off guard at this challenge coming from a girl. He laughed and walked away from her into his classroom. Meryl was upset by Lemar's reaction. She didn't want to fight him; she just wanted to get his attention. She had a secret crush on him but didn't know how to tell him.

Every day after that, Meryl taunted Lemar. "I want to fight you!"

Lemar replied, "I Don't fight girls." He thought to himself, *Girls only fight girls. Why does she want to fight me?* He later found out that Meryl had fought with a couple of the other boys in school and had won the fights. She was now picking on Lemar because her victories were making her bolder.

Still, Lemar couldn't see himself fighting with Meryl, although she antagonized him daily. *I Don't fight girls. I Don't know what I did to her. I Don't understand why she wants to fight me so badly*, Lemar thought. Meryl kept bothering Lemar day after day, saying, "I want to fight you!" But Lemar kept giving her the same answer, "I Don't fight girls!"

One day, after school, Lemar walked past an old dirt mound that led to the local bus stop. He saw Meryl in the mix of a small crowd of boys. She spotted him walking by and stared him down! The crowd was a combination of students from their school and kids from other neighborhoods. *She really is a tomboy*, he thought. Meryl stepped out of the crowd and headed straight for Lemar.

"You're going to fight me today!" Meryl said menacingly, teeth clenched as she approached Lemar.

"I told you. I Don't fight girls." He calmly replied.

As she walked toward Lemar, the crowd of boys and some additional onlookers began to parade behind Meryl.

"If I punch you in the face, you will have to hit me back," Meryl said to antagonize him.

"I Don't want to fight with you," Lemar stated and began to walk away before Meryl got to him.

Meryl pulled a boy from the crowd, "Well, then you're going to fight him!"

Athen emerged and stood with his fist balled, using his body language to threaten Lemar. The crowd parted as if orchestrated to do so. He stood directly across from Lemar. Lemar looked Athen up and down and thought, *Who is this boy? He looks too old to want to fight me. He's dressed like a man with a job.* Lemar noticed that Athen had a big square-shaped glass ring on one of his fingers, and his fist was balled tight. Lemar immediately realized he had no choice but to fight.

Hopefully, he wasn't carrying a knife. Lemar scanned Athen one more time. Knives were a normal part of the arsenal for a street fight. It was typical for young thugs in any neighborhood to carry all sorts of knives—long, short, or pocketknives. Lemar wasn't into that lifestyle and didn't carry a knife.

It was at that moment Lemar realized how serious Meryl had been about fighting him. But what confused him was why? They'd never had any issues or run-ins, and he didn't understand why she became so obsessed with fighting him. And why did she go to the extreme of bringing someone else to fight him?

Lemar dropped his book bag, stood his ground, and balled his fists in defense as Athen charged. Athen threw a couple of haymakers with his 'ring hand.' Lemar dodged the punches and then waited for Athen's next move. Athen jumped back away from Lemar, indicating he was afraid of Lemar, who was unfazed by his attack. He looked into Athen's eyes, and he saw that the fight was over.

Meryl chose a pretender instead of a real fighter. That's why he was so well dressed with the stupid ring on his finger. Lemar also realized at this moment that being compassionate didn't mean that he was weaker than Athen; in fact, he realized that it was strength. Lemar also didn't launch an attack on Athen because he knew he was outnumbered. He knew fighting a mob wasn't smart, especially if they were already carrying a bunch of pocketknives. That's when he looked over at Meryl with contempt.

He caught her gaze, and it was oddly pleasant. In fact, she was looking at him with some sort of admiration. He was confused, which made him even angrier at her. As he gathered his book bag, he backed away from the crowd but made certain not to turn his back on them. He didn't want to be caught off guard by one of the other boys, whom he believed may have been armed with a knife or weapon. Once far enough away from the mob, Lemar turned and headed for the bus stop. *I pray this doesn't get worse. I hope this is over now.* He pondered as he made his way to the main road for the bus.

Once safely on the bus, Lemar felt thankful for the courage he was able to display. He didn't want the confrontation to escalate. The next day as he arose from his sleep and prepared himself for school, all he could think about was the awkward look on Meryl's face after he'd fended off the assailant she sent after him. As he walked into the classroom, one of the first people he ran into was Meryl. She walked past him and smiled. Wait a minute! She just smiled at me. Lemar couldn't believe his eyes. He was still upset with her and too disgusted about her actions the day before and couldn't bring himself to smile back at her.

Lemar talked about the situation with his father's housekeeper Ms. Claudia. Lemar was afraid to tell his parents that he had been in fights at school. Over the years, he developed a strong bond with Ms. Claudia, especially after she set him straight about being bullied by Floyd and his father, the 'policeman.' He didn't understand Meryl's intentions or actions, but he knew he was very annoyed at her.

Ms. Claudia's explanation was similar to Viola's warnings, "Some girls who like you might not know how to approach you or express it, so they act in a way to make you believe they really Don't like you. Some girls want to be domineering and want to know the boy they like can handle it."

So, does this mean Meryl likes me? Ugh. I Don't like her like that now, not after what she did. From that day, Lemar would give Meryl a 'tight-lipped' smile whenever she smiled at him. She never challenged him to a fight again, and she just kept smiling at him.

CHAPTER 19

DADDY & DAUGHTER

Meshel was Celine's fifth child but the first child of her father, David. He was determined to make sure his baby girl was educated and given a chance to make something out of her life. At an early age, he pushed her to learn to read, learn the alphabet, count, and enjoy educational things. David's focus was zoned in on academics and less on socializing. He was usually not playful with his children, except at reading time with Meshel. Meshel was a bit shy, and ironically, she started learning to read into the inconsistencies of the grown-ups around her.

"Meshel, get your reading book and sit by daddy's lap. Read so that everyone can hear you." David often showcased his daughter's reading talent to his co-workers whenever they came over. He incentivized his colleagues by promising them "a drink" if they would assess Meshel's reading. Over time, their demand to hear Meshel read increased. David treated her reading sessions like a sought-after performance.

Meshel's reading advanced and flourished beautifully. By the time she was five years old, she was reading like an accomplished second grader, smoothly, with expression, and at a natural speed. Her articulation and pronunciation was superb. At times, the crowds of ten people or more boosted Meshel's social skills and confidence. She broke out of her shyness and developed a resonant voice, which would eventually lead her to be the most outspoken of her siblings.

Meshel's Uncle Greg recognized her improved reading ability, increased confidence, eloquence, and solid reading skills. She was articulate and didn't speak with a strong native accent, which made people listen even more when she spoke. Uncle Greg never wanted her to get into fistfights with other children, so he reminded her every time he saw her temper rising, 'Meshel, listen to me! Your words have way more power over these girls. Use your words!" She became the most vocal advocate and protector of her younger siblings, while her older siblings and other adults resented the sting of her criticisms.

Meshel once said to Celine, "Mammi, why you Don't clean the bathroom before and after you bathe just like Daddy?"

"Just like your blasted father!" Celine would say to Meshel, "Little Miss Clean. Everything you scorn just like your father."

Meshel learned her cleaning habits from her father, David. He would quickly clean the bathroom before and after he took his shower. It was his way of giving courtesy to the next person to use the bathroom after himself. Whenever he'd go clean the bathroom, Meshel would stand by the door and admire his diligence. They developed this routine where she'd ask, "Daddy, what are you doing?"

"Meshel, go and sit down." David would snap, though not too harshly.

Brave Meshel would stay put and ask again, "But what are you doing, daddy?"

"I'm cleaning the bathroom, Meshel." David would then pick his head up to look at Meshel, "go sit down and watch Sesame Street. He wasn't angry at Meshel because she asked, but he needed some privacy if she would go away just so he could smile about her cuteness and willingness to help. David's father was never affectionate to him or his older brother, who ran away and never looked back. This left David alone with his father to pick up the slack for work to be done at home. David felt betrayed by his brother, and this is why affection never came easily for David with his children.

"Okay, daddy," Meshel replied, but still, Meshel would smile and remain in the doorway until he was done.

This routine brought Meshel great comfort. She adored her father, even though he often hid his adoration in return. David brought calm, discipline, and stability to Meshel's life. She was very dear to his heart, which sometimes made Celine slightly jealous of their relationship. Meshel would often hear her complain and criticize him, "This man thinks he's so clean. All he's doing is teaching this child to clean and read. Just irks my blasted nerves! I need help with the bills. I need some cleaning money for the house!" It was clear that Celine was angry with David. She resented him so much that she never hid it from her children.

Celine worked two full-time jobs to support the entire family. She also sold knick-knacks and small treats she cooked at home. With so many children to clothe and feed, her jobs and side hustles still weren't enough to make ends meet. With the combination of stress from David's lack of financial contribution and her suffocated income, Celine resorted to undignified solutions.

CHAPTER 20

LITTLE SISTERS

Mr. Milton was one of Celine's old friends since childhood. Milton, unfortunately, had fallen on hard times. He played with the ladies at his civil service job for the government, where one of his female supervisors forced him to retire early instead of having him fired for cheating on her. She made sure to tarnish Milton's rapport within the agencies, which forced him to settle for a much lower paying desk-clerk position with a local newspaper Downtown. After that, Milton could only afford to rent a room but still drove his own car.

On the rare occasion when Celine went food shopping Downtown, Milton would often catch sight of her through the windows of his job. Celine was pleased with his attention, which started with offers of spending money, free car rides, and, eventually, his sexual advances. She was willing to ignore his present situation. She thought *Milton is giving me more than this worthless cheap-man David. Let me see if he will empty his bag for me.* Milton spent the bag on Celine and her older children but spent nothing on the younger ones. Celine made excuses for Milton's behavior, all for the sake of her benefit from his support.

Months later, Celine found herself pregnant! *Oh gosh!* She thought as panic set in. She had to find ways to cover her tracks because of David. She sent Estelle and Roger to stay with relatives while she pondered what to do with the rest of the children for the next few months.

Word traveled through town, and David overheard rumors

about Celine and Milton. Celine was already giving David the cold shoulder at home, which partially confirmed that the rumors were true.

She was very selective of whom she confided in, as she felt it was time that she and David had some space between them. "David, I want to fix up the house, and I Don't want the children to be in the way."

David was shocked, though not completely surprised. "I fixed the van to run it as a taxi, so I could make money to help with the bills. When will you finish?"

"A few weeks, David." Celine was short with her answer.

A few weeks?" Her response caught David off guard. Then continued his probe, "Who's doing the work? Who's paying for it? Where are we staying?"

Celine rolled her eyes. She was annoyed by his interrogation. She held back her impulse to blurt out her real intention. She didn't want to create a fuss in front of her children, although they were no strangers to her fierce rants.

"I'm paying for it!" Celine snapped and continued, "I did what I had to so I could get the money to fix my house. You been cleaning house, but you too slow to fix things. The house has been falling apart! And you never have any blasted money! So, you can go stay with your sisters, and I'll go with the children to Herman's. Maybe you can drop the children off at Herman's house with the van?"

David paused and held his composure, "That's why I fixed the van, to drive it as a taxi and make some money to help you out."

It's a little too late for that! Where was the help a few months ago? Celine wanted to shout but held back her thoughts. "Well, I want to fix it now. I Don't want to wait."

"Why can't I stay with you and the children at Herman's?" David questioned.

Celine reminded him, "You know Herman is a Christian, and he doesn't approve that we sleep together unmarried. He doesn't care that we have children."

"So, I'm supposed to be away from all of you for weeks?" David turned and walked away, unwilling to argue with Celine and secretly believing that the rumors about where she was getting her money from were true.

David wasn't happy. He did not want to be away from his children for any amount of time. But, after they packed up, he drove them to Herman's house before heading to his sisters'. He assured the children he would stop by as often as he could. Celine stood with her arms crossed, ready to rid herself of David. She felt a tinge of sorrow for her children, but it wasn't enough to make her change her mind. After all, she had fallen in love with Mr. Milton and was ready to forge ahead with their relationship.

She was headstrong in executing her plan to separate from David.

She did her best to avoid seeing David while at Herman's so he couldn't see her growing belly. Although David suspected something peculiar, he didn't press Herman whenever he turned him away from his home. Herman suspected his sister was deceitful and disagreed with her illegitimate pregnancy, but he didn't express his dissent for the sake of his nieces and nephews.

Her children would often nag her to see their father. "We miss daddy. We miss daddy! When are we going home?" they would complain. Celine was exhausted from their grumbling and too tired to discipline them, so she'd give a dry response, "Your father and I need some time to ourselves right now. You all will see him soon."

David attempted to visit his children frequently but was often met with resistance. It broke his heart, and he grew angrier each time he was turned away. These are my children! These people can't keep me from my children! His contempt for Celine festered. He knew she was hiding something but never thought she might be carrying another man's child. The rumors that she was running around with Mr. Milton began to give him pounding headaches.

One evening while driving his taxi, David spotted Mr. Milton standing with a group of mutual friends. Milton's eyes stretched open as if he had seen a ghost as David jumped out of his van and approached the group. David shook each of their hands, and when he got to Milton, he stood in front of him, sizing him up from head to toe. Milton trembled at his knees. He stuck his hand out to shake David's hand. David didn't know all the details of what was rumored about Milton and Celine, but by Milton's nervous behavior, David suspected there was some truth to the gossip. He gripped Milton's hand, leaned in, and whispered in his ear, "Make sure you stay clear of my children. You hear me, player?" Milton grimaced as David released his grip.

Celine's belly rounded out as the months passed and protruded through her clothing.

"Mammi's pregnant!" Meshel said to Pamela.

"I know," Pamela replied. Pamela knew Celine was pregnant before her siblings because Celine confided in her one evening. She swore her to secrecy with a promise of a special favor.

"But why are we here? Why Mommy and Daddy not together? They're not happy about the baby?" Meshel questioned Pamela.

"I Don't know," Pamela shrugged.

"Obviously, you Don't know what you should know!" Meshel snapped at Pamela.

"Whatever!" Pamela snapped back.

"Well, I want to see daddy!" Meshel snapped as she walked away from Pamela with tears in her eyes.

Neither of them understood why they couldn't see David.

They didn't understand why Celine avoided talking about him or answering their questions to see him. They wondered why she didn't talk about her obvious pregnancy and why their uncle Herman held a shameful demeanor towards his sister. They also missed Estelle and Roger. There was so much unknown, and both Meshel and Pamela were annoyed with Celine for creating such confusion. But because they knew better than to go against their mother, they began taking their frustration out on each other.

When Celine gave birth, seven months had gone by since she'd left her home and David. Some work had been done on her home while they were away, but the house remained empty most of the time. David continued his quest to visit his children and was now void of any desire to have a relationship with Celine. He'd heard more rumors of Celine and Milton's relationship and decided to let her be.

A'lynn and A'sharia were now the youngest children in Celine's clan. They were twins, and they were the spitting image of Mr. Milton. Meshel, Pamela, and Roland, their youngest brother, were all shocked to greet their new baby sisters, who didn't resemble David at all, whom they believed was the twins' father as well. Their confusion intensified, but they dared not ask Celine any questions.

"They Don't look like Daddy!" Meshel uttered to Pamela quietly one night at bedtime.

"Meshel, I can see that!" Pamela whispered.

"Where they came from? Whose babies did Mammie bring home?" Meshel asked.

"I used to think daddy was their daddy too. I think I heard Uncle Herman complain to Mammie about some man named Milton. He must be their father." Pamela shared.

"I heard Uncle Herman too. That's why he was always vexed." Meshel confirmed.

Meshel and Pamela lay quietly in their bunk beds. Shocked at their discovery. Upset at Celine. And sad for David. Meshel desperately wanted to see her father so she could hug him and tell him he was still her favorite person.

CHAPTER 21

UNCLE VEE

After the Meryl Fessit incidents, Lemar wanted a male perspective on how to deal with the young ladies. Ms. Claudia gave Lemar her view of Meryl's crush on him, but Lemar was still traumatized and went to his uncle Vee afterward to get the male side of things. Earl was not the birds-and-bees discussion type; he would only leave little magazine clues around the house for Lemar to find and figure things out on his own.

One afternoon after school, Lemar was home and heard Uncle Vee playing records from his collection in the back of the house. Lemar walked through the sliding glass doors from the front porch and found Uncle Vee wearing headphones, cueing his mixer down. Uncle Vee was Lemar's first teacher in the role of the 'Disc Jockey.' On Lemar's last count, there was a collection of over six-hundred-thirty-eight old-school vinyl discs immaculately kept, with music from Bob Marley to the O'Jays, and then some. Vee selected an exceptional Jazz album called "Cherry," he meticulously wiped off the disc and blew off any dust before laying it down and posting the needle to release some smooth Jazz. Lemar always recalled the smooth saxophone section by Stanley Turrentine; he remembered the cut because it was later used on one of the hardest rap songs he'd ever heard on Boogie Down Productions, "My Philosophy."

Uncle Vee was the ladies' man, so Lemar was intent on learning a thing or two about how to handle boyish-girls and girly-girls. He was already not fond of tomboys like Meryl, so after sitting down on a crate near Vee, he asked, "Uncle Vee, how do I know if a regular girl likes me?"

Vee was perplexed, "What do you mean by 'regular' girl, Lem?"

"I mean, a girl that's not a tomboy," Lemar quipped, smirking at the puzzled wrinkles over his uncle's eyebrows.

"What happened? Some girl beat you up or something?" Vee asked, now smirking back at Lemar.

"No, uncle, but this girl at school wanted to fight with me because she was beating up other boys. Then when I told her I Don't fight girls, she set me up to fight some outside boy after school. The fight was quick, and I left her, the boy, and a whole crowd behind without getting beaten up. But the next day, she started smiling at me a lot. Ms. Claudia says she was just testing me because she likes me. Testing me? I Don't trust her! So I want to learn about regular girly-girls."

Uncle Vee laughed uncontrollably. After he regained his composure, he said to Lemar while chuckling. "Girly-girls will test you as well, nephew, it just won't be so violent per se, but they're going to test you as well."

Lemar looked disappointed. "Uncle Vee, that's not funny; why is it even regular girls want to test you?"

"To make sure you're worthy of their 'liking you,' my nephew. Their feelings for a boy or a man is their treasure. They want to make sure the boy or man has the right keys for their treasure. Get it?" Uncle Vee was no longer chuckling; he now had a more rigid look while staring at Lemar for a response. *You'll get it in time, little nephew*, he thought.

Lemar hesitated… "Okay, Uncle Vee. I get it, I Don't really like it, but I get it." *Why can't they just like me if I like them? What's with all this drama?* Lemar thought as he walked away from Uncle Vee towards the sliding glass doors at the front of the house. BLAM!!!

Lemar walked smack into the sliding glass door face first and hit his forehead. Stunned and dazed, he wondered why he didn't see the glass in front of him and reached up with his hand to feel his forehead for a lump or some blood on his face. Uncle Vee heard the impact and ran from the back of the house after pausing the music. He saw Lemar standing in front of the glass door, looking stunned. He realized his confused nephew had walked smack into the glass and was about to cry from the shock and shame of being so clumsy.

Vee held his nephew and patted him on the back, "Hush, nephew, you're not bleeding; you're alright." Lemar leaned on his uncle for a few seconds to gather himself, then said, "I didn't see the glass, Uncle Vee! Thank you." This time uncle Vee slid the glass doors open for Lemar and watched as his nephew walked through to the front porch. Vee shook his head and walked away to get back into playing his music. On the other hand, Lemar had a headache and a nice lump on his forehead.

Later that afternoon, Earl saw Lemar's lump on his forehead. Vee had informed Earl of Lemar's little accident, so Earl said while bursting at the seams to hold his laughter in, "Lem! Go put some ice on your cocoa," that meant ice for the coconut lump on his forehead. Not wanting to miss the opportunity to joke about his nephew's mild misfortune, Uncle Vee played a loud song for Lemar to remember. He found an album by Lionel Richie and played the cut "You're once - twice - three tiiiimes a laaaady, and I loooove youuuu." Earl heard the music and laughed; Lemar heard it and was annoyed. He hid in his room while thinking, Why did Uncle Vee have to play that song? That's messed up.

CHAPTER 22

MEMORIES OF DAVID

"Mammi, can we go home now?"

"Hush, children! Don't you see I have to take care of your little sisters?"

"But Mammi, we miss daddy!"

"Settle down, children. It's going to be fine!" Uncle Herman chimed in. He felt sorry for his nieces and nephews. He watched his sister deceive her children as she attempted to get them to forget their father.

Celine never directly admitted to her children that the twins were Mr. Milton's children. However, by this time, the rumors of Celine and Mr. Milton's relationship had spilled into Uncle Herman's home. Anytime guests were over for bible study, Celine would be the center of discussion. Meshel and Pamela would hide behind the wall in the living room and quietly listen in on the conversations. Herman no longer tried to defend his sister. His disdain for her situation was evident, and he openly shared his feelings with his church friends. Celine didn't care what her brother or his church friends thought about her; all she cared about was being able to hide out at his house while she avoided David.

Once Herman found out that Milton had been sneaking into his house to see Celine and the twins, he could no longer allow her to stay at his house. He wasn't a fan of David, but he despised Milton. He came to Celine one evening and said, "You have to go! I can no longer have you here while that man comes creeping at my back door."

"Herman, what do you want me to do? He is the father of my daughters." Celine retorted.

"I Don't care. You wouldn't let David come see his children, but you want me to let this man come here while the other children suffer from not seeing their father?" he responded.

"I Don't want anything to do with David. You said you didn't like him anyway because he didn't marry me. So, why do you care?" Celine argued.

"These kids Don't have anything to do with you not wanting David. That's their father, and he deserves to see his children! And I rather David than that creeping man, Milton!" Herman admitted. He was frustrated with his sister Celine.

"Well, I guess I will pack up and go!" Celine replied. She was annoyed with her brother for not accepting Milton.

A'lynn and A'sharia were about three months old when Celine packed up all her children to go home. Herman hugged his nieces and nephews as they piled up in Milton's car. He saw the sadness on their faces as they realized the rumors about their mother were true. They didn't want to leave their uncle and didn't want to go anywhere with Mr. Milton.

"Don't worry, children. The Lord will bless you." Uncle Herman tried to reassure them.

Meshel looked out the rear window with tears rolling down

her cheeks as they drove away from her uncle's house.

Halfway to their house, Celine called for her children's attention. "Children, I have some bad news to tell you."

They were all silent, awaiting her next words.

"Something has happened to your father." Celine shared.

"What happened?" Meshel found herself asking. Pamela and Roland were shocked at the boldness of her question and the tone she used with Celine.

Celine darted her eyes in Meshel's direction, threatening her with her stare. Meshel immediately boiled down, turning silent again, listening for Celine's answer.

Pamela grabbed both Meshel and Roland's hands for strength. They all fixed their eyes on Celine.

"Your father was killed." Celine let out the words.

"What?" Meshel, Pamela, and Roland all said in unison. They all began sobbing and consoling one another. "What happened to him, Mammi?" Pamela spoke out this time, not waiting for Meshel to ask.

"I'll tell you all later," Celine replied as she turned her back for the remainder of the drive home.

When they arrived at Celine's house, Meshel exited the car first and stepped into the yard. She smelled a horrible stench and saw dried blood stains in the front yard. She halted, in shock, at the odor and sight of the dried blood.

"Mammi, what's this?" Meshel demanded.

Celine remained nonchalant, "It's your father's blood. He was killed here, Meshel."

"What? Who did it, Mammi?" Meshel continued.

"Your father and your uncle Greg's friend got into a fight, and your father got hurt and died," Celine answered as if she was telling her children what was on the menu for dinner that evening.

"Why were they fighting? Why did he kill my father? Do we have to stay here? Meshel demanded.

"I Don't know, Meshel. I Don't know anything about what your father was doing. He never did anything for all of you anyway. And, yes, we are staying here. This is our home!" Celine snapped as she stepped over the blood stain, A'lynn in hand, and headed into her house. Milton followed behind with little A'sharia in hand.

Meshel, Pamela, and Roland stood in the yard and consoled one another.

The next day, Estelle and Rodger both came home. Celine wanted to control the narrative for her younger children before the older ones were told. Now Estelle and Roger were told about the tragedy and brought up to speed.

Celine refused to allow any of her children to attend David's funeral despite their aunt Grand-aunt Doris' pleas.

"Celine, please, let the children go to their father's funeral," Doris pleaded.

"No. My children won't be going!" Celine insisted.

Initially, Meshel believed that her mother was protecting their feelings. After all, they hadn't seen David for over six months, and she figured her mother didn't want them to see him in such a way. But Meshel soon found out that Celine's intentions were just purely selfish. She wanted her children to rid themselves of David just as she had. She wanted to build a life with Milton.

After the funeral, Aunt Doris visited Celine and the children. The police gave her David's belongings, and she found a five-dollar bill in his wallet with Meshel's name written on it. Doris wanted to be sure Meshel got the money and knew that if she had given it to Celine, Meshel would never see it. So, on her visit, she pulled Meshel to the side, slid the five-dollar bill in her hand, and whispered, "I found something for you from your father's wallet after he died." She had seen David's body in the morgue, and the police had given her the contents of David's pockets from the crime scene. "Meshel. I found this in your father's wallet. Keep it. It's for you. And Don't tell anyone."

"Thank you, Aunt Doris," Meshel said as she hugged her grand aunt.

Celine spied their encounter and waited for Doris to leave before approaching Meshel.

"What did she give you?" Celine asked.

"Nothing. Just something from my father." Meshel stuttered. "Show me!" Celine insisted.

Meshel opened her hand to expose the neatly folded five-dollar bill.

"Hand it to me." Celine demanded.

"But it's mine. My father left it for me!" Meshel's voice cracked as she answered her mother.

"Give me that money. He never did anything else for me, so that's mine!" Celine snatched the five-dollar bill from Meshel's hand and continued, "I need to buy a pack of cigarettes anyway."

Meshel went to hide in her private spot behind the house and cried. She missed her father and began to hate her mother.

Celine's children were deeply saddened and tried to console one another. They would huddle together for hours and reminisce over stories about David. They all missed him dearly and were aligned on their disdain for their mother and Milton's behavior. The older children hardly ever interacted with the twins. Celine adorned the twins with most of her attention as she desperately wanted to feel like a family with Milton.

One evening, Meshel waltzed into her mother's room, seeking to find some comfort from her, only to find Celine and Milton hugging, kissing, and fooling around. Celine eyed Meshel as she pulled back the curtains looking for her mother.

"Meshel, you're supposed to knock!" Celine scolded.

Meshel was angry; she couldn't believe what she was witnessing, so she snapped at Celine, "Knock on what, Mammie, the walls. There's no door, just curtains!"

"Go outside! … I said go Outside!" Celine demanded.

Meshel rolled her eyes and walked away. She heard Milton laugh out loud as Celine attempted to "hush" him up. *He seems so creepy. I Don't trust him.* Meshel thought. She suspected that he had something to do with her father's death but didn't have any idea how to prove it. She knew, however, that she would have to keep a keen watch on Mr. Milton.

CHAPTER 23

NIGHT BY THE OCEAN

After David's death, the children stayed home from school for two months. Once they returned to school, the teachers were quite fascinated to hear their stories over and over again. The teachers weren't truly empathetic towards them; they just loved to hear about the drama and the shame happening in Meshel's family! Pretty soon, Mammi found out that she was the local talk of the town and forbade the children to discuss the story anymore in school, or else!

Mammi also told Meshel and her siblings not to cry anymore because David never did anything for them. She tried to force her children to live in her world of imagination.

After David's death, Celine immediately moved on with her new relationship, and she was not interested in the approval of her children. She was then openly immersed in a relationship with Mr. Milton. Meshel thought, *'was she already with him while with my father?'* Concluding that this had to be accurate and not just a mere possibility, Meshel became outraged and infuriated! She could only watch as this 'new man' moved into their home. All her siblings were upset except for Pamela.

Mr. Milton wasted no time establishing his presence and exercising his authority in Celine's home. "Mammi, let this man move in with us, and he has no respect!" Meshel complained to her brothers and sisters. Meshel was nine years old and grew increasingly tired of Mr. Milton's presence and habits.

Milton would take over the television with the remote and

change the channel to his shows amidst their shows just because he could! He would accuse Meshel and her siblings of not having respect for him! However accurate (or inaccurate) it may have been, Celine was standing by her man's side! The twins were, of course, neutral territory; everyone loved them! They were born two months before David died.

Celine never seemed to openly defend her children against Milton, "Oh gosh! Never mind that!" she often said. She constantly tried to appease their anger toward Milton. Even Estelle went against Celine, asking, "Are you stupid or what? One man just died, and you're already with another one so fast?" There were times Milton denied Meshel's oldest brother food, and he spanked her younger brother on a whim, just because he could! From the onset, Meshel's blood did not take to Mr. Milton, and now her blood was boiling against him!

Mr. Milton was thought of as a shady character. Although he had the attention of both Celine and her brother Greg, it seemed he had another agenda. Celine was simply too in love to see objectively, and Greg was so supportive of Celine that he might not have thought about it either, or so it seemed. It seemed there was no wrong that Milton could do, of course, if Celine told the story. Celine's children had complaints rather than compliments for Milton, but there was one questionable night where driving near the ocean spoke volumes.

"Children, Let's go for a ride!" Celine said to Meshel, Pamela, and little Roland, who all hesitated. They whispered amongst themselves while still in the other room, "Why does she want us to go in Mr. Milton's car with her? He doesn't even like us!" "You hear me, children? Let's go!" Meshel, as usual, was the first to speak out, "Mammi, I Don't want to go." "Meshel! Hush your mouth and do as I tell you! All of you get in the car, and we're going for a ride." "And it's already evening time; why are we going out so late?" whispered Pamela to Meshel. Little Roland remained silent as he often did. He didn't want any more chastisements from Mr. Milton or Celine.

The three sat next to each other in the back of Mr. Milton's car as they drove off under the late evening streetlights. Celine was seated in the front passenger side, looking like she was deep in thought the entire time they drove. After about an hour, Mr. Milton finally stopped at a stretch of road called Pointe-A-Preen. Pamela knew the place because she had been there with Celine and Mr. Milton a couple of times before. Both Celine and Mr. Milton got out of the car. Celine said, "We'll be back!" Then she and Mr. Milton walked off into what seemed to be total darkness. Pointe-A-Preen had high tides in the late evening, and it was rumored that cars would wash away into the deep ocean nearby on rare occasions.

"Why are we here?" Meshel said, then turned to Pamela and asked further, "Pamela, you think they want to kill us?"

"No," said Pamela, "Mammi wouldn't do that to us!"

Meshel would not take no for an answer, "but why are we here then?" she kept repeating. Pamela was annoyed and afraid. Little Roland sat in complete silence. He felt cold from fear and tucked himself under his sister Pamela's side. Meshel said, "This place is dangerous at night, and Mammi let Mr. Milton bring us here?"

Pamela became concerned that Meshel was making sense, but she kept answering, "Meshel, Mammi wouldn't do that to us!"

Finally, after about twenty minutes, Celine and Mr. Milton emerged from the darkness, strolling towards the car. Celine seemed very stressed, while Mr. Milton seemed moderately upset. It was apparent to Meshel and Pamela that there was some tension between the adults; perhaps they argued for a while in the darkness.

From that day, the children were convinced that Mr. Milton tried to persuade Celine to leave them to die at Point-A-Preen in the car during high tide, but Celine refused. She returned to the car and didn't utter a word the entire way home. Mr. Milton did not say a word either. Meshel always wondered. 'Was he trying to get rid of us that night?'

Celine was the first to get out of the car at home, but she didn't go inside. "Children, go inside."

All three children quickly got out of the car and ran into the house, huddled in Meshel and Pamela's room. Pamela said to Meshel, "See, I told you Mammi wouldn't let that happen to us!"

Meshel responded, "It felt like the first time Mammi showed a conscience since Daddy was killed."

Celine then came into the house. "You children, get ready for bed!"

"Yes, Mammi," was the unanimous reply. All three were exhausted from the strange ordeal, and little Roland finally broke his silence and asked his sisters, "can I sleep with you all tonight?" They said, "Yes, you can. We won't tell Mammi."

CHAPTER 24

SUMMERTIME

School was over, and it was summertime. After a once-in-a-lifetime trip to Disney World with Mrs. Sherry and her son Lance, Lemar was set to spend the balance of his summer break with his father's parents, Aunt Milly, and his cousin Royce out in the countryside. As he spent his traditional summer holidays with his grandparents, his always welcomed trip slowly turned from Disney glows into countryside woes. Summer with his grandparents was usually uneventful, but this summer visit proved to be quite the opposite.

Lemar's grandparents lived under humble means. Although they had electricity in their house, the darkness at night was thick outdoors, with the exception of two dim streetlights near his grandparent's house and the occasional light shining in the distance from each home. Therefore, Lemar was usually in the house as soon as the sun set for the evening. They didn't own a television, so the only entertainment was Grandpa Franz's battery-operated radio, which he kept on the stations he liked. Nights were boring for Lemar, and he often was left to find ways to keep himself entertained.

One evening, Lemar was bored and restless as the day cooled off. He was desperate to find something to do, so when cousin Royce announced he would visit Aunt Milly in her new apartment, Lemar was eager to tag along. Royce wasn't particularly happy to have his little cousin join him for the walk. The terrain and darkness were a bit hectic for him at night, let alone having Lemar trail him, which would make the journey much more difficult. The roads were winding, poorly paved, and edged with steep cliff-like precipices on one side; missteps could lead to falls into oblivion with a possibility of fatality. Nevertheless, he reluctantly agreed to let Lemar accompany him on this journey.

"Alright, put your shoes on; come on, hurry up!" Royce snapped at Lemar.

"Ok." Lemar didn't pay any mind to Royce's tone; he was simply too happy to get away from the house for some excitement.

It was still late evening, so the orange skies of twilight cast their amber glow over the last-minute journey to Aunt Milly's apartment flat. Aunt Milly greeted her son and nephew, fed them, and soon after, Royce announced his intention to return home to his grandparents' house for the night. Royce issues a reasonable choice to Lemar, but again the stubborn little tag-a-long chooses to ignore sound advice. "Stay with Aunty until the morning, and I'll come back to get you after breakfast," Royce stated.

Even the fresh breakfast option wasn't enough to convince Lemar he should stay overnight. Lemar wanted the adventure. "No, I want to come to grandma and grandpa's with you."

Royce, highly annoyed thought. *This little boy doesn't like to listen.* "Alright then. Come on, let's go."

The reality of the extreme darkness at night hit Lemar like

a ton of bricks just a few yards past the last streetlight. His vision was challenged, as he couldn't see his hand in front of his face. He reached out for Royce's hand but couldn't find it. Royce's pace picked up the moment they were engulfed in the darkness. Through a combination of stretched steps and speed walking, Lemar desperately tried to keep up with his cousin.

"Royce, please slow down. I can't see, I can't see you!" Lemar called out into the darkness. His plea was met with silence. He called out again, "Royce, please slow down; I can't see you!" Still no response. Lemar's heart began to pound. He wondered if he had made Royce upset by not listening to his advice. He was afraid but tried to convince himself that 'Everything's gonna be alright' like Bob Marley sang. Royce takes this walk all the time; nothing ever happens to him. He was snapped out of his thoughts by the sound of Royce's shoes scraping the pavement and disturbing pebbles and pieces of crumbled pavement. That was Royce's way of telling him where to walk on the dark road.

"Royce! Royce!" Lemar called out again. Royce still didn't answer. *I'm telling Aunt Milly as soon as I see h*er, Lemar planned. Soon there was a glimpse of light in the far distance. Lemar's lungs re-filled with air, and he let out a loud, long sigh. He no longer needed Royce's guidance. He followed the light from the house like a star guiding him to his final destination. As the light replaced the darkness, Royce's shadow emerged. Lemar rushed ahead to pass Royce and beat him to the doorstep of his grandparents' house.

Lemar knew why Royce was so mean to him; he knew he should have listened. Nevertheless, he was still upset with his big cousin. They had a decent relationship, and he looked up to Royce. But for some reason, that evening, he felt like Royce didn't care for him tagging along.

Once they were back at his grandparents' house, Lemar washed up and changed his clothes for bed. Royce hopped into the big bed they shared as if nothing ever happened. Lemar pulled this cover over his head and didn't say one word to Royce.

Lemar was awakened in the middle of the night by the sound of rain thumping on the zinc roof. The sound of the rain was comforting to Lemar. He peeked his head from beneath the covers and saw that Royce was still sound asleep. Every night Royce would take the side of the queen-sized bed next to the wall and tease Lemar, "I got the corner, ha!" As he stuck his tongue out at Lemar like the middle-finger gesture. Tonight Royce did not tease Lemar as he usually did, but it was Lemar's turn to get revenge for what Royce had done to him earlier that night.

He inched over between Royce and the wall, then pressed his feet up against Royce's back, legs outstretched until he pushed Royce off the bed. THUMP!! Royce hit the floor. He woke up dazed and confused. However, he didn't suspect that Lemar had shoved him off the bed. He got up and hopped back in bed. Good for him! Lemar silently chuckled with his head under the covers.

Both boys woke up bright and early in the morning. Royce complained about his elbow hurting and couldn't understand how he had a golf ball-sized knot on his elbow. Lemar's joy of revenge quickly turned to guilt. Although he was upset with Royce for ignoring his fear of the dark while walking from Aunt Milly's house, he didn't like seeing his cousin hurt. *Oh, boy! Maybe I shouldn't have pushed him off the bed.* Lemar pondered. Should I tell him I pushed him off the bed? Lemar gave serious thought to confessing. However, he opted not to because he didn't want to feel the wrath of his grandfather's belt. Instead, he waited hand-and-foot on Royce over the next two days until his conscience felt better.

CHAPTER 25

PREDATOR

❝I'm so sick and tired of him; he's evil!" Meshel complained about her stepfather, Mr. Milton. "He's always starting trouble, and Mammi never defends us." Meshel knew very little about David's family and wished she did so she could go and live with them. She once heard about his two sisters. She recalled her father saying, "One of them is blind, but she's still very independent." David often told Meshel that she shared many of his family's features and looked a lot like his sisters. He talked about how calm and laid back his sisters were and always stopped short of comparing Meshel's attitude to theirs. Celine would boast that Meshel shared her temperament. David often agreed. However, he went to great lengths to try and teach Meshel how to practice self-control and use her words wisely.

Meshel and Celine's personalities were so similar that it was an open family agreement that 'this' was the reason why they didn't get along most of the time. "Two bulls can't live in the same bullpen," Brownie would say.

Meshel wasn't trying to be her mother's ruler or equal. She didn't intend to be disobedient or disrespectful. However, she often felt she needed to defend herself and her younger siblings, a challenger to her mother's inexcusable behavior when it came to Mr. Milton. Additionally, she could not sit for Mr. Milton's assertion of himself over the household her father once led. He was authoritarian, pushy, demanding, lazy around the house, and often creepy, so unlike her father, David.

As Meshel and Pamela grew older, Mr. Milton began stooping to new lows. They would catch him peeping on them while changing their clothes in their room. Pamela never complained about his peeping because she didn't want to hurt Celine's feelings. Celine and Pamela shared a special bond, and Celine often bragged about how much she and Pamela resembled each other. Meshel often wondered if her mother disliked her because she looked so much like David.

"He's such a creep, looking in on young girls! I'm going to tell Mammi about her creepy man!" Meshel said to Pamela.

"No, Meshel. He's just old. Let Mammi be happy with her man." Pamela pleaded.

Pamela's passive attitude about Mr. Milton made Meshel's blood boil. Meshel couldn't understand how she could be so nonchalant about it. Why does she care to spare Celine's feelings when Celine clearly doesn't care about ours? Meshel often wondered.

"Well, if you are okay with Mr. Creepy looking at your panties, that's your burden!" Meshel lashed out.

"Meshel, now you know I'm not okay with that. I just Don't want to hurt Mammi's feelings." Pamela pleaded her case, not wanting to tell their mother of Mr. Milton's behavior.

"Well, I'm not sparing her feelings because she doesn't spare ours!" Meshel's mind was made up that she was all-in on pulling back the curtains on Mr. Milton and Celine's precarious relationship. She didn't share with Pamela that she was also concerned that Mr. Milton's peeking would turn into something more sinister and wicked, and she wanted their mother to open her eyes before one of them was violated.

One day after catching Mr. Milton sneaking a peek at Pamela while she was in the shower, Meshel went on a rampage. She went straight to her mother and demanded that she put him out.

"He's a creep! He's peeking at your precious daughters! You Don't see you need to put him out?" Meshel demanded.

"If you Don't like him, then 'you' can always leave!" Celine retorted.

Celine's response shocked Meshel and sent her running off in tears. *She doesn't even care that he's making a peepshow of her daughters. What kind of mother is this?* Celine didn't bother to address Meshel's concerns, and she didn't confront Mr. Milton. What was most surprising to her was that her mother never made any attempts to keep a watchful eye on Mr. Milton. So, Meshel took her complaint to her uncle Greg, but he didn't bother to look into it either. She felt like she was on her own and grew increasingly weary of Mr. Milton. Estelle and Roger were older; they rarely spent time at home, almost always staying with older relatives. Pamela didn't seem to care much, and Roland was too young to say or do anything. Meshel decided to set out on a quest to find out more about her father's family. Her goal was to get out of her mother's house and Mr. Milton's predatory territory.

Meshel began to ask her mother about her aunts casually. Celine was surprisingly receptive and freely shared some of the information she had. Meshel quickly learned that Celine didn't like David's sisters very much. She felt like they thought they were better than her, although they often sought money and help from her and David. As Celine shared with Meshel, she also complained about all the support and sacrifices she felt compelled to make so they could travel and pursue their endeavors. The expectation David's parents put on him to take care of his sisters somehow became Celine's responsibility at a time when she was in love with him. Now she resented David's whole family and felt like they limited her opportunities. Celine was so entrenched in her complaints that she didn't realize she'd given Meshel one crucial piece of information; one of her aunt's addresses.

Meshel felt an inkling of sympathy for her mother. She didn't realize how much Celine had given up on David to support his sisters. Meshel's perception of Celine changed slightly because she saw how hard her mother worked. However, she never knew that Celine's past efforts were for the benefit of others. But she also learned that what she already suspected was that Celine, although outspoken and shrewd, was a follower and a people pleaser. It became more apparent to Meshel why her mother had submitted to Mr. Milton.

Meshel's sympathy for Celine didn't last long. It was upended one evening when she noticed Mr. Milton creeping around her and Pamela's bedroom late one night while they were sleeping. She heard the floorboard creak, and when she opened her eyes, there he was, making his way toward Pamela's bed. Meshel was surprised at his audacity but equally afraid of his presence in their room. She wanted to scream for her mother but decided against it. *She won't believe me anyway, even if she caught this man in our bed.* Meshel thought. So, she ruffled her sheets with her feet and slowly rose from her bed. Mr. Milton was startled and rushed out of the bedroom. Meshel got out of bed and walked to the bathroom, pretending to use the bathroom. She looked around to ensure the coast was clear and went back into her bedroom. She quickly closed the door behind her and pushed the rickety rocking chair up against the door.

"Pamela! Pamela!" Meshel forcefully whispered her sister's name. Pamela didn't budge. Meshel lay awake in her bed, with tears streaming down her cheeks until she dozed off to sleep. She didn't know that Pamela was also awake in her bed, quietly shivering as she lay in a pool of her own tears. She was glad Meshel saved her from the dirty hands of Mr. Milton.

CHAPTER 26

THE PREY

The morning after Pamela's close encounter with Mr. Milton, Meshel decided she had to leave. She could no longer live in fear of Mr. Milton or the disgust of her mother's ignorance. She wanted to ask Pamela to leave with her, but she knew Pamela was too loyal to leave their mother. So, Meshel kept her plans to herself and began planning her escape.

One morning while Mr. Milton, Celine, Pamela, Roland, and the twins went out for a long ride, Meshel decided to journey to the address Celine had given her. She pretended she had her usual bad monthly cramps, so Celine let her stay home. "But didn't you just have cramps three weeks ago, Meshel? Okay, alright, stay home until we get back." Celine relented, not wanting to argue again with Meshel at that moment. Meshel left five minutes after they left and arrived at the well-maintained home. She knocked on the door, and a beautiful, statuesque woman came opening the door; her face lit up as soon as she saw Meshel.

"My gosh! Look at you! You look just like your father!" The woman, immediately recognizing Meshel, said. "Come inside! Come inside!" she urged.

Meshel was pleasantly surprised to be recognized so easily and welcomed so warmly.

"I'm your Aunt Kay. I'm so pleased to meet you, Meshel." she smiled and said. "Your father, David, talked about you children all the time."

Meshel smiled jovially. She had just met her aunt but felt like she loved her already. Meshel's eyes scanned the house as she followed her aunt into the kitchen. She noticed pictures of her father framed and hung on the walls and on the tables and consoles. She was also surprised to see photos of her younger self framed and posted throughout the house. She spotted a picture of herself, Pamela, David, and Estelle sitting in the sand on a crowded beach. She and Pamela were maybe three and two years old each, both holding hands, while Estelle and David loomed over them in the background, smiling. Meshel found herself thinking about how happy they looked. *I wish those days were here now*. She thought to herself.

"Have a seat, Meshel." Said Aunt Kay, pulling out a chair at the kitchen table.

"Thank you," Meshel obliged.

"I can't believe you're here!" Aunt Kay exclaimed, but her excitement immediately turned to concern. "Does Celine know you're here? Is everything okay?"

Meshel looked up at her aunt, her eyes turning red as she held the tears in, "No. Mammi doesn't know I'm here. I Don't want to go back there! There's so much going on. I'm afraid. I just can't stay there." Meshel revealed as she began sobbing.

For hours, Aunt Kay sat and listened to Meshel's horror stories about Mr. Milton and Celine. She felt enraged with Celine. She also felt sorry and slightly afraid for her nieces. She didn't say it out loud but thought. *My brother would kill that man for messing with his girls!* Aunt Kay fed Meshel and let her take a nap for a little while before it was time for her to head home.

"Don't worry, Meshel. We will figure this out. I'm going to talk to your Aunt Desiree when she gets home. Make haste and come back here tomorrow, okay." Aunt Kay instructed.

Meshel went home that afternoon, thrilled about having met her aunt. Somehow it made her feel closer to her father. She thought about the pictures she saw of him, her, and her sisters and how happy they appeared. She smiled at her aunt's beauty and was even happier when she looked in the mirror for their resemblance. She wanted to tell Pamela but felt it was best to keep this secret visit to herself. She did all she could to avoid Mr. Milton and Celine for the rest of that evening.

Pamela snuggled under her covers as she watched Meshel slide the rocking chair in front of their bedroom door. She didn't question her sister. She fell sound asleep, knowing she was safe under Meshel's protective measures. Meshel crawled into her bed, eager to see her aunt the next day. Meshel was too excited to sleep that night. On top of that, she wanted to keep an eye out for peeping-creeping Mr. Milton.

The following day, Meshel hopped out of bed but then made an excuse to her mother to leave the house. She got dressed and made her way to her aunt's house. *Hmm, the little wretch is feeling better already?* Celine thought. When she arrived, her aunt Kay informed her that her aunt Desiree wanted to meet her. Meshel had never been around a blind person before and was slightly nervous. However, she was surprised at how well her aunt moved around. It didn't seem like she was blind at all.

Aunt Desiree was just as beautiful as her aunt Kay. Meshel thought that Aunt Desiree looked a lot more like David than Aunt Kay, although they all resembled one another. Aunt Desiree was much blunter than Aunt Kay. While she was warm and comforting towards Meshel, her tone was much more fiery when she spoke about Celine and Mr. Milton. Meshel enjoyed learning about her family from her aunts. She was excited to know that she belonged to educated, successful, and apparently, less dramatic people. Their lives were in stark contrast to the life Meshel had come to know living with her mother and Mr. Milton. Her aunts helped her devise a plan to move in with them. They were also open to Pamela coming, but Meshel knew it would be near impossible to get Pamela to leave Celine. She worried about what would happen to her sister once she was gone, but Meshel knew she still had to get away.

"Take this with you. Keep it in your pocket and sleep with it under your pillow!" Aunt Desiree said, handing Meshel a small pocketknife. Meshel was shocked; she learned about violence after bullying Beverly in school and seeing her father's blood on the ground.

"No, thank you, Aunty, I can't do something like that; that's not me, but thank you," Meshel said, politely decrying her aunt's offer.

"But child, how will you stop him if he persists?" Asked Aunt Desiree.

Meshel explained to her aunt, "I'll just keep putting the rocking chair behind the door handle. If he gets in, it's because he has to make a lot of noise, and everybody will have to take notice of what he's doing."

"Okay, Meshel, I see you have a plan." Said her blind aunt. "But keep your eyes open with this old pervert, eh! Don't let your guard down. You hear me?"

On the day Meshel was set to tell Celine that she had met her aunts and planned to move in with them, she spent hours rehearsing the conversation. Celine was sitting in the living room, putting A'lynn and A'sharia to sleep for their afternoon nap, when Meshel came in and sat next to her. Perfect timing! Meshel realizes. She has the babies, so she's not likely to be able to go off on me.

"Mammi, I need to tell you something," Meshel spoke softly, beginning the conversation.

"What is it, Meshel?" Celine asked calmly, making sure not to disturb the twins, rocking their cots.

"I met my aunts, Desiree and Kay," Meshel said hesitantly. "Okay. And?" Celine responded.

Meshel took a big swallow to remove the lump growing in

her throat. "I'm going to go and live with them." She winced nervously after the words came out of her mouth.

Celine's ears perked up. She seemed excited! Meshel was confused by her reaction and thought she must have misread her mother.

"That's good, child. But remember, you must treat your aunts with respect and follow their rules." Celine instructed.

Meshel was so ecstatic that she jumped up and hugged her mother before running off to pack her clothes. *That was easier than I thought. Damn? You're so happy to get rid of your child. Most parents would fight, but whatever. Bye!* She thought to herself while she loaded her bag. Meshel didn't spend much time questioning why her mother didn't challenge or outright forbid her from moving in with her aunts. She was more focused on the fact that she was getting out of her mother's house, away from the unhappiness, and no longer having to sleep with one eye open to watch out for Mr. Milton.

Pamela overheard Meshel and Celine's conversation as she hid behind the curtain to the hallway to listen in. She followed Meshel into their bedroom as Meshel ran past her to pack her things.

"Are you really leaving Meshel?" Pamela asked.

"Yup! You can come if you want too as well. Aunt Desiree and Aunt Kay said you're welcomed too," Meshel offered her sister.

"Are they really nice?" Pamela inquired.

"Yes, Pam. They are sooo nice. They look sooo much like Daddy too. They are beautiful!" Meshel exclaimed.

"I'm going to miss you," Pamela said, indirectly letting Meshel know she would not be joining her.

"I'm going to miss you too, Pam. I just can't stay here with that man anymore." Meshel said.

"I know. Trust me, I know." Pamela responded.

Meshel walked over to her sister, hugged her, then reminded her, "remember to put the rocking chair behind the door handle every night. He can't come in unless he causes everybody to hear him breaking the door. Then everybody will know about him, and Mammi can't deny he's a pervert after that."

"Okay, Meshel, I will. I love you, sis'" Pamela said.

"I love you too, Pam," Meshel replied. They hugged each other tightly and cried a little on each other's necks, wiping the tears off their own faces as they parted.

Meshel felt as if she had died and gone to heaven. Not only was she going to be getting away from living under the same roof as Mr. Milton, but she was also going to be living with her father's family, and she was especially going to see her brother Roger more often since he still visited Aunt Desiree from time to time.

As she got to know her aunts better, Meshel came to know how close they were already with Roger but not so much with Estelle. Estelle was closer to her and Roger's father's family as she got older, while Roger was not so close; he kept his distance from his father's family and preferred the family of Meshel's dad David instead. Aunt Desiree ran a successful business and taught Roger about the business and how to manage money. Meshel was a little annoyed that Roger had not told her that he was so close to her aunts. *Why didn't Roger tell me that he was so close to Aunt Desiree and Aunt Kay?*

CHAPTER 27

VIOLATED

Lemar began spending more time with his Aunt Milly. Initially, he'd stay the weekend at her apartment; then, he began spending entire weeks with her during his visits to the countryside. After graduating from the regional university, Milly secured a good-paying job with the Department of Education. Now, she had the funds to host Lemar for the entire summer if she chose, and he leaped at the opportunity. She also hosted one senior student for the summer holidays, always a female, in her home. This was her way of giving back to the less fortunate and encouraging her students to have hope for their futures. Milly always secretly screened her students during the school year and even had private discussions with the family involved whenever she was close to making her final decision on who the lucky girl would be. This summer, that girl would be a sixteen-year-old named Mitzy.

Milly was a stickler about reading, good grammar, a clean house, and good manners. She often corrected Lemar and Mitzy's grammar if they mispronounced words or used words out of context. When Lemar stayed with her, she made sure he followed a rigid reading plan; one summer, he read through two sets of encyclopedias and an entire collection of books on fairy tales. Lemar was often found lying on the cool, ceramic-tiled floor with a book in front of him. Milly enjoyed seeing her nephew's love of reading.

Milly was a modest and quiet woman who spent most of her free time alone, with her student, and with Lemar when he visited. She never hosted overnight visitors otherwise and rarely had anyone over during the evenings. So Lemar was surprised one night to wake up to his aunt in their shared room with a strange man he couldn't clearly see because of the darkness and poorly lit room.

"Aunty Milly, who is that?" Lemar asked his aunt.

"Relax, sweetheart. Go back to sleep or go in Mitzy's room and sleep." She tried to sound calm, but her voice shook with nervousness.

Lemar sensed her nervousness and probed, "Are you sure you're, okay?"

The stranger leaned in and whispered something in Milly's ear, and she urged Lemar, "Yes. I'm okay. Just go in Mitzy's room."

As Lemar backed out of his aunt's room, he saw a light reflecting off a long blade in the man's hand. Then he saw his aunt raise her nightgown and lean back against the wall. The stranger stepped in front of her and lowered his hands in front of himself. Lemar heard the sound of a zipper and saw the stranger's pants drop around his ankles. Milly and the stranger didn't realize that Lemar was still peeping into the room through the dim light of her kerosene torch lamp. The tall shadow pressed his body against Milly's and began moving his hips back and forth in a jerky pattern. Milly turned her face away from the stranger and saw Lemar standing at her doorway. Tears streamed down her face. Lemar felt helpless and whimpered. And just as fast as he began, the stranger was done when he heard Lemar. He then took his knife, pointed it at Milly, grabbed her by the wrist, and guided her toward her bed. Lemar watched them walk slowly across the room. His eyes were fixed on the knife in the stranger's hand.

"Go in the other room, I said!" Aunt Milly frantically commanded him. She was under pressure, and Lemar was annoying her by not listening at such a time of critical factors.

Lemar finally gave in to her instructions. He went into Mitzy's room and woke her up. He explained what he saw in Aunt Milly's room, then they both sat up, contemplating ways to defend his aunt against the knife-wielding intruder. They were snapped out of their huddle by a scream, so they ran to Aunt Milly's room, this time ready to spring into action, but quickly realized the scream they heard was that of the intruder. They saw the strange man holding his eyes, stumbling around the room, his knife swinging at anything in his path, and tripping his way out of the window.

"Aunt Milly! Aunt Milly! What happened?" Lemar and Mitzy tried to rush into her room as she rushed to push them both out while she was on the way out herself.

"I got him!" Milly exclaimed, "I poured turpentine into his face! I'm sure he's blind because I definitely got it in his eyes!" Milly further declared.

She grabbed Lemar and encouraged Mitzy to come along as they all ran next door to her neighbor's door. The neighbors overheard the man's screams and opened the door as they arrived, and they immediately dialed 1-1-9 to call the police.

Once the police arrived, Milly told them of the ordeal she faced. They also took a statement from Lemar and Mitzy since they witnessed the incident. Lemar sat in shock, cuddling with Mitzy, as his aunt explained the details of what took place. His heart sank when he heard her say, "I was raped." He felt sad for his aunt and ashamed that he couldn't do more to help her thwart the attack. Mitzy simply gasped and broke down into tears; she already understood what rape meant.

"I think I may have blinded him," Milly told the police officer. "I had no choice," she repeated, "I had no choice."

"Don't worry, miss. You won't be in any trouble," the police officer assured her.

Lemar, Milly, and Mitzy stayed the night at the neighbor's house; they were too shaken up to return to Milly's apartment. They all snuggled together on the sofa until morning.

CHAPTER 28

DISCOVERIES

Meshel and her Aunt Kay proved to be good with each other. Meshel was happy to have someone to look up to, and Kay was thrilled to have someone young to be around. Aunt Kay shared her many life lessons and experiences with Meshel, and Meshel was an eager to learn student. She finally felt loved and cared for again. They spent time baking, and Aunt Kay showed Meshel all her baking secrets. They talked about boys, and Aunt Kay often gave Meshel great advice on how she should expect to be treated by a boy, lessons David taught Aunt Kay when she was young. They even spent time talking about local and national politics, which helped to broaden Meshel's perspectives and outlook on the world, lessons that would benefit her in the future. Aunt Kay learned from Meshel as well. She learned how to be strong and speak up for what she believed in. Aunt Kay was tepid, which was the main difference between her and Aunt Desiree, who was more passionate about life.

Meshel began to thrive after she moved in with her aunts. Over the next couple of years, her grades in school soared. She seemed, overall, happier. She and Pamela were still very close, and they saw each other every day at school. Celine even let Pamela come over and visit Meshel. Pamela kept Meshel informed about things happening under Celine's roof and kept Celine informed about Meshel's well-being. Meshel was relieved that Pamela managed to keep Mr. Milton at bay after she kept the bedroom door blocked with the rocking chair at night. One night after Meshel was gone, Milton did indeed try the door to the bedroom, but upon finding it blocked at first, made a mild stir asking, "Why is this door blocked?"

Pamela remained under covers, modestly worried as she thought, *Oh gosh, this man is really trying to get in the room with me. Meshel was right. Let me see if he's stupid or what? Make some more noise so Mammi can hear you. You blasted pervert!*

"Pamela! Open this door," he whispered as he wrung the door handle like an addicted fiend looking for satisfaction.

Pamela became enraged! She echoed some of Meshel's spunk and leaped out of her bed, throwing off the covers mid-air as she arose. "If you Don't leave me alone, then I'm going to tell my brother Roger. He will deal with you, he and his crew."

Milton was caught off guard. Roger was in his early twenties, and some of his guys were well-known ruffians. He thought, *there's no need to stir up a nest of hornets by myself.* "Okay, Pamela, I was just checking on you. Have a good night," he whispered through the door.

Good riddance! Pamela thought. She refused to give Milton any verbal response to his obvious lie! She walked back to her bed and pulled the covers up to her neck like the cape of a super-heroine; *I fixed him good tonight!* Pamela thought.

A week later, as Meshel and Pamela were walking to the grocery store, Pamela told Meshel about Mr. Milton's failed attempt and how she fixed his perverted tail. "Good! Said Meshel. "Roger's guys would definitely fix him good!" Then Pamela seemed particularly interested in hearing more about the lessons Aunt Kay shared with Meshel about boys.

"Meshel, does Aunt Kay let you go out often with your boyfriend?" Pamela asked.

"No, she won't let me go out with him much. I spend most of my time baking with Aunt Kay or helping Aunt Desiree," Meshel admitted.

"Doesn't your boyfriend get upset?" Pamela asked.

"No. He doesn't seem to be upset." Meshel answered. "Why are you asking these questions, Pam?"

Pamela sighed, "Well, my boyfriend is alright, but I Don't know if it's going to last."

"Why? What happened? Meshel inquired.

"Well, he's like you. He doesn't come out much. You know I like to go out and dance. But he doesn't want to." Pamela shared. "Oh!" was all Meshel could think to say.

"He's nice and all. He treats me good because I demand the things Aunt Kay taught us. But I think I want something different," Pamela admitted.

Meshel nodded and said, "Well, Pamela, I hope you find what you're looking for. Just Don't make the same mistake Mammi made."

Meshel liked her boyfriend, but it didn't matter much if she didn't see him often. He liked her, and he was kind. She also liked him but had a hard time trusting him. He hadn't done anything to break her trust, but after losing her father and dealing with Mr. Milton, Meshel was a little traumatized. She'd known pure love from her father, but it was snatched away all too soon. She'd also witnessed deceitfulness masked as love by Milton towards her mother, Celine. Both situations brought immense heartache and pain and allowing herself to immerse herself in a relationship proved to be too much at the moment. So, Aunt Kay's and Aunt Desiree's needs and wants of her time were her way to avoid really committing emotionally to any boyfriend.

Aunt Desire began dating one of her colleagues from the school where she taught. Mr. Myrie was one of the staff members at the school where she taught. He was the Director of Transportation. Although she was blind, he had grown fond of her. She was quite an attractive woman with a great mind for teaching visually impaired students. Mr. Myrie admired her tenacity and her physical beauty. He wasn't what one would consider a handsome man. He took great care of himself but was often overlooked by women because of his looks. So, the reciprocated attention he received from Aunt Desiree was gladly accepted.

When he brought Aunt Desiree home, Mr. Myrie was impressed to find a household full of beautiful women one evening. Meshel and Aunt Kay warmly welcomed Mr. Myrie as they were thrilled to see how happy he made Aunt Desiree. Having no reason to feel vulnerable whenever he would visit, Meshel went about her normal activities around the house. She'd take care of her chores, bake with Aunt Kay, and assist with whatever Aunt Desiree needed her to do when asked. However, one evening while Meshel was sweeping, she noticed Mr. Myrie staring at her. It creeped her out because she recognized that same stare from Mr. Milton. She tried to shake it off since he often only seemed interested in asking her about school and her plans. After she'd answered his questions, he'd turn his undivided attention to her aunt Desiree.

"Pamela, I have to tell you something," Meshel confided in her sister during one of her visits. "I think Mr. Myrie's been looking at me just like Milton did to us at Mammi's house."

Shocked and in disbelief, Pamela responded, "Meshel, you're kidding me? Are you sure?"

"All I know is every time I catch him looking, he starts asking me questions about school and stuff," Meshel explained.

"Did you tell Aunt Kay?" Pamela asked.

"I can't tell her. What if she's like Uncle Greg and turns against me? I'm only telling you, Pam." Meshel spoke in fear.

"I don't know what to tell you, Meshel. Where else would you stay if you can't stay there?" Pamela inquired.

"I don't know, Pam. I don't know." Meshel said as she signed. *Why is this happening again?!* She thought to herself.

"I'll pray for you, Sis," Pamela assured her sister. Pamela worried even more for her older sister. She knew Meshel would never return to their mother's house while Mr. Milton was still there. Yet, If Mr. Myrie continued his behavior, she would not last at Aunt Kay's and Aunt Desiree's.

Meshel somehow convinced herself that perhaps Mr. Myrie was genuinely interested in her future and school. After all, he did work in a school himself. She decided to test her theory by asking him a few questions one night while he was visiting.

"Mr. Myrie, I want to be a nurse. Since you work at the school and are around nurses all day, do you know how long it takes and how much it costs to become one?" Meshel asked.

Mr. Myrie responded, "Well, Meshel, I only deal with transporting the students and teachers, so I Don't get to see the real details of how long it takes or how much it costs to study nursing."

"Oh, okay. I was just wondering if it would take long and cost a lot. I Don't even know how I would pay for it anyway." Said Meshel, baiting him into her trap.

Mr. Myrie, like a hungry shark, took the bait, "Well, Meshel, I'm sure a pretty girl like you can find a man willing to pay for you to go to school."

Meshel raised an eyebrow but didn't respond.

"I'd certainly pay for a pretty girl like you to go to school."

I knew it! I wish it wasn't true, but I knew it! Meshel cringed.

Meshel didn't know her Aunt Desiree was listening in on their conversation. Aunt Desiree's preferred narrative was, Meshel is flirting with my boyfriend, not that Mr. Myrie was attempting to seduce her niece. Even though she couldn't see how Mr. Myrie looked at Meshel, she sensed his distraction whenever Meshel entered any room, they were in. Aunt Desiree didn't speak a word about her jealousy to either Meshel or Aunt Kay. She instead decided that she would keep Meshel busy enough to be out of the sight of Mr. Myrie.

The next day while Meshel was at school, Aunt Desire called out for Aunt Kay.

"Kay! When Meshel gets home, I want her to do some chores for me," She ordered.

"Okay, Des. But she already does plenty of chores around the house." Kay reminded her sister.

Aunt Desiree ignored Kay and continued, "I want her to have enough chores to keep her busy! Especially when Myrie is here!"

Aunt Kay raised an eyebrow and questioned. "What does Myrie have to do with anything?"

"Don't worry about it. Just have Miss Lady organize that messy shed outside by the side of the house." Aunt Desiree insisted.

"The shed? It's been years since anyone has touched that mess." Aunt Kay rebutted.

"Exactly! And now she will do it." Aunt Desiree responded firmly.

"Des, you're something else sometimes. No problem. I'll help her." Aunt Kay replied.

"No! No! No! I don't want you to help her. She can do it on her own." Aunt Desiree persisted.

"This seems like some sort of punishment, Desiree. What did she do? I hope this doesn't have anything to do with Myrie. If his eyes are wandering, it is not that child's fault." Aunt Kay confirmed what Desiree had hoped not to be true of her boyfriend.

Aunt Kay gave Meshel her instructions when she arrived home, and Meshel obliged. She was okay with the task as she wanted to be as far away from Mr. Myrie as possible. She also saw it as an opportunity to learn more about her father's family. Meshel knew how people liked to keep all their memories and secrets packed away in their sheds. *Ooooh, this will be like a treasure hunt for me! I'm excited.* She thought.

Meshel's hunt paid off. She found pictures of her father and aunts when they were young. They looked like they were very close, always smiling and laughing in the photos. Meshel was surprised by just how much her Aunt Kay looked like her. She appeared to be the spitting image of Meshel, and if one didn't know, they could easily be mistaken for the same person. David and Aunt Desire looked like they could have been twins, except he was about five inches taller than her.

"Hmm, I see why Mammi fell in love with my father; he was handsome!" Meshel said out loud to the ears of the four walls of the shed. There were pictures of David and Celine, young, carefree, and happy. They made a handsome couple since they were both extremely good-looking. Meshel found pictures of Celine when she was pregnant and tried to guess which child, she was pregnant with during the time. There were also pictures of Celine and her aunts. They looked like they were the best of friends. In some of the pictures, Meshel could see that Celine and her aunts were dressed alike. They all looked very happy. Wow, they used to be really close. I wonder what happened? She found images of her brother Roger as a little boy held by Aunt Kay with her aunt Desiree standing next to them. Then she came across a few pictures that nearly made her fall to her knees. In the picture were her aunt Desiree and Mr. Milton. They were hugging each other with big loving smiles on their faces. There was another with her aunt sitting on his lap, and he was kissing her cheek. There was even one with her aunt Desiree and Mr. Milton, Celine, and David, her uncle Greg and a woman she'd never seen before, and her aunt Kay with a friend of her father's that she used to see when he visited their house. All the women were standing in front of their partners, with arms wrapped around their waists.

Meshel was floored. She grew even more curious to learn about all their histories. Evidently, their stories and lives intertwined, and she wanted to know how. *How could my aunt have been in a relationship with the same man my mother is now shacking up with? How could Aunt Kay be connected to the man who was accused of killing my father?* It was all confusing yet intriguing to Meshel, and she wanted to know more.

CHAPTER 29

SURPRISE

Mr. Myrie began to notice that he saw Meshel less and less when visiting Aunt Desiree. He didn't want to spark Desiree's curiosity, so he didn't say anything initially. However, one evening, his curiosity got the best of him, and he asked Aunt Desiree, "Where's your niece? I haven't seen her in a while."

Aunt Desiree was annoyed at Mr. Myrie for asking about Meshel. She snapped at him, "She's doing a project for me in the shed."

"Perhaps I should go out and check on her and see if I can offer her any help." He proposed.

Aunt Desiree was not happy about his enthusiasm to help Meshel, and she didn't want him to know she was insecure about the attention he paid her niece, so she reluctantly agreed to him checking on Meshel. "Okay, suit yourself. Don't take long; we have dinner to eat."

Desire barely got the words out of her mouth before Myrie headed out to the door to the shed. He turned back and shouted a quick, "Okay, my dear. I'll be back to eat."

When Myrie got to the front door of the shed, he was surprised at the mountain of boxes and old furniture neatly placed throughout the space. Meshel had carved out an aisle for walking through the mounds of stuff. Myrie didn't see Meshel as he eyed the space. He called out her name, "Meshel, are you in here?"

Meshel was startled by Mr. Myrie's voice and dropped the

pictures she had in her hand. *What does he want?* She thought to herself and rolled her eyes. She picked up her head, slightly visible behind the boxes she was busy organizing, and answered, "Yes. I'm here. Is everything okay with Aunt Desiree?"

"Everything is okay. Your aunt asked me to come out and check on you," he lied.

Meshel was pleased to see him for a brief moment, believing that her aunt cared enough to send someone to check on her. She smiled at Myrie and waved him over to where she was.

"Cheese-on-bread! There's a lot of stuff in here." He said as he made his way to the back of the shed where Meshel was working.

"Yes, it is a lot of stuff. But I'm making sense of it so that it's organized for my aunts." Meshel happily bragged.

Myrie noticed some large boxes and an industrial-sized sewing machine off in the corner. He pointed at the items and asked, "What about that stuff?"

"Oh, yea. I need to get to that, but it's too heavy for me to move on my own." Meshel said.

"Well, I can help with that." Myrie offered.

"Great!" Meshel exclaimed. She stood up and stretched her legs across the boxes to make her way to the sewing machine. "We should move this first."

Myrie admired Meshel as she moved about. He noticed the curves in her hips and her silky skin. He found himself very attracted to her. She reminded him of a younger version of her aunt Desiree. *She's such a beautiful girl.* He thought to himself as he met her by the sewing machine. Myrie wasn't normally impulsive, but something came over him at the moment. When he got closer to Meshel, he grabbed her hand and asked, "How do you feel about older men?"

Meshel snatched her hand away and said, "I think they should date older women."

Meshel's response didn't dissuade Myrie. He persisted, "I like you a lot. You remind me of a younger version of your aunt Desiree. You're very beautiful and smart. I can give you anything you want." Myrie thought if he complimented her and made an offer to the young girl, she would be willing to succumb to his wishes. He was wrong.

"I knew you were no good for my aunt. I saw the way you looked at me. I'm disgusted by men like you. You need to leave now before I tell my aunt about your nasty behavior!" Meshel said, careful to keep her voice down, so her aunt did not hear her.

Myrie was embarrassed. He was also worried that Meshel would expose him to her aunt. He tried to recover by saying, "I'm sorry, Meshel. I didn't mean any harm. I wasn't trying to come on to you." He also knew how strongly Desiree felt for him and dared to say, "I Don't think it's a good idea to tell your aunt;

she won't believe you anyway."

"You're a liar! You knew exactly what you were doing. Just leave this shed now!" Meshel stepped over a few boxes to distance herself from Myrie.

Myrie turned away and headed out the door and back to the house. He didn't say another word to Meshel as he exited.

Once upstairs, Myrie sat next to Desiree and put his arm around her. She nestled her head into his shoulder and asked, "How is Meshel?"

"She's good. She doesn't need my help." He replied.

It's men like that that made me move out of my mother's house. Now I have to deal with it here? Why can't they just leave me alone so I can have some peace? Meshel sobbed quietly as she continued her work in the shed.

Meshel decided to tell her aunt Kay what happened with Mr. Myrie. She was surprised when her aunt hesitated to believe her. Kay warned her against telling her aunt Desiree because she knew Desiree could be vicious when she felt like someone, she cared for was being attacked. Kay knew how much Desiree cared about Myrie, and nothing anyone said would change her mind. Meshel didn't listen and decided she would tell her aunt about the bad-behaved vile man she was with.

When Desiree arrived home that evening, Meshel was eagerly awaiting her. Aunt Kay listened in from another room of the house, sure to be far enough away from the ensuing drama.

"Aunt Desiree, I have something to tell you," Meshel said.

Desiree assumed Meshel would complain or give her news about the mounds of items in the shed. She navigated her way to the sofa and parked her walking cane as she sat to listen to her niece. "What do you need to tell me, Meshel? Did you find something in the shed you need help with?"

Meshel took a swallow and sighed, "I hate to tell you this, aunty, but Mr. Myrie made a pass at me in the shed the other day."

"Well, Meshel, sometimes, an old man needs some fun on the side to be sure they still have a desire for the one they truly love." Desiree's response surprised Meshel. She continued, "He's good to me, and I'm not letting him go."

Meshel's jaw dropped. Her aunt didn't care one bit about the inappropriate behavior of Mr. Myrie. She seemed to expect it and was okay with justifying it. She didn't show one bit of concern about how uncomfortable it made Meshel. Meshel couldn't catch her breath quick enough to respond. Her eyes filled with tears, and all she could think was, I want my daddy.

Desiree stood up and said, "Meshel, I think it may be best if you leave. We've enjoyed your time here, but I Don't want to have you around, Myrie, anymore."

Defeated, Meshel responded, "Okay, Aunt Desiree, I'll leave."

Meshel felt helpless and heartbroken. Her aunts knew why she left her mother's house, and they were furious to hear about Mr. Milton's creepy ways, so why was it okay for Mr. Myrie to behave that way? Meshel couldn't understand. She felt isolated and violated; she wondered how she always ended up being the villain in these situations.

CHAPTER 30

UNCLE GREG

Meshel wondered if she'd ever find peace and a place to live that was a safe haven. She'd been stripped of her safety and comfort when her father died. Her mother and aunts left her 'cat-spraddled,' feeling stretched out and discouraged from their failures to protect her innocence. They chose disgraced men over her. They proved too weak and insecure to cut these men off after showing their desire to take advantage of young girls, especially young relatives. I will never be so weak and insecure. These nasty men will never control my mind to make me overlook their disgusting ways. Meshel made a pact with herself.

Nevertheless, she was now faced with the dilemma of going back to live with her mother and Mr. Milton. The thought made Meshel sick, and she decided to try another route and ask her uncle Greg if she could stay with him instead.

Meshel wasn't sure she could trust her uncle because she knew he backed whatever bad decisions Celine made. He was also friends with Mr. Milton and thus far unwilling to believe Mr. Milton would go after his nieces. Additionally, she often wondered how much more he knew about her father's death. However, staying with her uncle was just external heat compared to the blazing fire waiting for her if she returned to her mother's house.

Meshel explained to her uncle what took place at her aunt's house. He didn't seem too interested. Meshel wasn't looking for his defense; she just needed him to understand that she needed a place to stay since she couldn't stay with her aunts anymore. Greg agreed to have Meshel stay with him but forewarned her that the decision wasn't his alone to make.

"Okay, Meshel, but you know I live with my girlfriend, Tryphena. I will have to speak with her first, but I think it should be okay. Just let me confirm first."

Tryphena felt sympathetic towards Meshel. She didn't say much to Greg, but she knew his niece's hardships and felt sorry for the young girl. Tryphena and Greg didn't have much and knew they wouldn't be able to care for Meshel indefinitely. They were willing to allow her to stay for the short term while she gathered herself after the incident at her aunt's house.

Greg allowed Meshel a few days to settle in before sitting her down to talk. "Meshel, Tryphena, and I don't have much, and it will be hard for us to take care of you."

Meshel felt the anxiety building up in her chest. She knew where this conversation was headed and wasn't ready for it.

Greg continued, "I will speak with your mother to see if you can go back home. That's where you belong. You are sixteen now and need space, and we don't have much space here. You also need a woman's guidance, and that's what your mother is for."

Meshel sighed. There wasn't anything she could do. She held back her tears and said, "Okay." *What kind of guidance can Mammi give me? She can't even guide herself.*

The next day Greg told Meshel that her mother Celine was okay with her moving back home, but there was one main condition; she would have to "respect Milton."

"Why do I have to respect that foul man? Obviously, Mammi doesn't see how he's been hurting her children. She needs to get him out of her house! Uncle Greg, why can't I stay with you?" Meshel begged.

"Meshel, I can't take care of you. If you Don't want to go home, then you may have to stay in a shelter for young women." Greg suggested.

"A SHELTER!" Meshel was devastated! "Is that really all you can do for me, Uncle Greg? After what happened to my father? You know how much I suffered!" Meshel cried, as her words left Uncle Greg startled.

Greg was caught off guard by Meshel's reference to her father and the insinuation regarding his death. She figured out that he was there when her father was killed, and that was the reason why he went to jail being charged as an accomplice, but Greg wondered, how much does she really know?

There was no room in Greg's home, and although Tryphena could be a stubborn woman, she was still more compassionate than Celine, Aunt Desiree, and Aunt Kay; she stood her ground with men, never allowing them to walk over her. She wasn't naïve like Celine, nor was she desperate like Desiree. Meshel believed Tryphena was just the type of woman who would be able to ensure no other predator would hunt her as their prey.

CHAPTER 31

THE MARRIAGE

Charlston Lloyd was a technology teacher at the university in the capital. He lived down the road from Celine's house and spent most of his time commuting to work at the university. However, whenever he was home, he could be found sitting on his porch just reading a book. He seemed fairly quiet but was always friendly with everyone in the neighborhood.

After leaving her uncle Greg's house, Meshel reluctantly moved back in with her mother. Pamela was thrilled to have her sister back home. While Meshel was happy to be with her sister again, she was never at ease knowing Mr. Milton was a couple of rooms away.

Meshel and Pamela walked past Charlston's house every morning and afternoon as they went to and came from school. They waved and smiled whenever they saw him sitting on his porch. Charlston took notice of Meshel from the first time he saw her. He had seen Pamela before and always thought she was a pretty girl, but Meshel really caught his eye. Initially, he was too ashamed to make any advances at her because he was much older and hid his feelings from Celine, with whom he had had many casual conversations. But Celine, while walking past his house and being a mother, never missed anything; she saw that Charlston had an eye for Meshel and asked him, "Seems like you like Meshel? I would love to have you for a son-in-law but proceed at your own risk; she is a little hellcat when she's ready. But my heart tells me you would take good care of her."

Charlston smirked. He detected a tinge of jealousy in Celine. While he certainly thought that Celine and Pamela were very beautiful, Meshel had caught his eye. Celine had just begun initiating a deal to pass her daughter off to this newfound friend. She looked past Charlston and noticed how clean his yard and the front of his house was. She figured he was older than Meshel but wasn't quite sure how much older.

"Are your parents home?" Celine inquired.

"No. I live here alone. My parents died a few years back." He shared.

"Sorry to hear that. Do you have any other family? Do they live here?" Celine probed.

"Yes. I'm very close with my aunt, my mother's sister, but she lives in the United States with my sisters and brothers." Charlston answered.

"Oh. How many sisters and brothers do you have?" Celine continued.

"There are five of us." He replied.

Charlston was strategic in answering her questions. He was sure to answer her specific question with a specific answer. He didn't divulge any additional information outside of what she asked for. He often used this tactic whenever someone wanted to understand why he stayed in the country instead of taking the opportunity for a better life with his family in the United States.

A few years back, Charlston made a questionable deal with a local shaman for the promise of prosperity. The dodgy exchange required Charlston never to leave the country, or he would lose his fortune and any other gains he made. Charlston loved money and his family, but this deal forced him to choose between his family and his wallet. His greed won the battle.

Celine and Charlston arranged for a meeting with Meshel. When Celine approached Meshel about meeting Charlston, Meshel was skeptical. *Why does she want to introduce me to some man?* She thought to herself. However, Meshel agreed as long as Pamela could join them. Celine decided that she'd combine their trip to the local shop with their visit to Charlston's; this way, she would avoid a conflict with Milton.

Charlston greeted Celine, Meshel, and Pamela with a warm welcome and offered them a seat on his porch. He presented himself gentlemanly and set out a tray of cold refreshing coconut water. They engaged in small talk and niceties. He asked Meshel and Pamela about school and their future plans. After about forty minutes, Celine reminded them that she needed to head to the local shop.

"What are you planning to buy, Meshel?" Charlston asked her.

"Um. I'm not buying anything." Meshel responded.

Charlston peeled off a few dollars from a wad of money he pulled from his back pocket, "Take this and buy yourself something nice. Be sure to share with your sister."

Meshel was caught off guard by his gesture. She looked at Celine for assistance on how to respond, and Celine stared off into the distance, pretending not to notice. Then Meshel looked at Pamela. Pamela smiled and said, "Miss Lady take the money; you might need it to do your hair later!

Meshel took the money from Charlston's hand and said, "Thank you."

"My pleasure. Feel free to let me know if you ever need anything else." Charlston didn't act thirsty, but deep down inside, he was happy as this was a win for him.

When they got home later that evening, Meshel asked Pamela, "Do you think Mr. Lloyd likes me?"

"Meshel, he said you can call him Charlston. And yes, it's obvious that he likes you." Pamela giggled and asked, "What are you going to do?"

"Do? Me? I'm not going to do anything. I Don't know what kind of person he is!" Meshel rebuked.

"But he seems so nice, Meshel; at least you know he's kind," Pamela added.

Meshel chuckled, "Pamela, please. I'm not thinking about that man like that. He's well established, yes, but obviously, nobody wants him."

Pamela giggled; she knew her sister well. She watched Meshel scope Charlston up and down while they were on his porch. He was nice-looking, well-dressed, intelligent, and financially stable.

They both laughed. Meshel admitted, "He may be a little cute. But he still has to prove himself."

"Hmmm. Meshel, you never know!" Pamela teased.

"You know what, Pam? I'm tired of talking to you. You sound like you Don't have much sense, eh!" Meshel snickered as they headed toward their bedroom.

Celine overheard their conversation and laughed to herself. She loved her daughters' relationship, although they had very different personalities. She was always close to Pamela but never really had a great relationship with Meshel. Meshel was a daddy's girl and spent nearly all her time with David when she was young. Celine felt guilty about not being more of a comfort to Meshel when David died, but she was too stubborn to admit it to her daughter. She thought the best way to repay her daughter for the agony she'd grown up with was to try and marry her off to a man who could provide for her.

Once they were in bed, Celine peeked her head into their room. "I hope you girls have been keeping your young legs closed, eh?"

Meshel and Pamela were caught off guard by Celine's question.

"Yes, Mammi, of course," Meshel responded.

Pamela replied with a dry "Uh-huh. Yes, Mammi."

As soon as Celine left their room and closed the door, Pamela and Meshel both covered their mouths simultaneously; they couldn't help their snickering and giggling at the thought of Mammi's words, "keeping your young legs closed."

CHAPTER 32

DIVORCE

The day Viola told Lemar that she would be moving overseas, and he would be living with his father full-time was one of the worst days of his life. At that moment, any hopes he had of his parents getting back together were severely crushed. She explained that they would still be as close as they always were, but for Lemar, it still felt like he was losing his mother and his first family. Admittedly, Lemar remembered how his mother tried to rekindle a relationship with his father. However, Earl was either too proud or too hurt or maybe just too stubborn to give their relationship another try. He didn't seem to be able to get past Viola's public flirtations and extravagant partying.

Earl and Viola both agreed that it was best for Lemar to stay with Earl while she took the time to regain her footing. They also believed that it was better for a boy to be raised by his father, a father who could teach him how to be a man. Lemar didn't mind living with his father, but for some strange reason, he felt like he didn't know him very well. He grew up splitting his time between his mother's and his father's homes, but most of his time was spent with his mother. Now he felt some solace since Royce had moved in with Earl a few months earlier. So Lemar wouldn't be alone. In as much as Lemar recognized Royce had authority over him, he still loved being around Royce.

Royce and Lemar shared a room and bed. They were used to sharing both since it was the same structure when they stayed with their grandparents. The boys often fought over who would get to sleep by the wall on the bed whenever they stayed at their grandparents, but there was no need for such a fight at Earl's since the bed was set in the middle of the room, Although Lemar was no stranger to sharing a bed and room with his cousin, this was the downside of not living with his mother, where he had his own bedroom and his own bed. Lemar mused, I'm going to miss having my own bed.

He quickly realized there was a lot he needed to learn about living with his father. Royce made it a little easier for Lemar to feel alright at home. He brought Lemar up to speed on a few of his father's strict rules. "First, Keep your grades up in school at all times, nineties if you can. Don't fool around with your school-work. No backtalk; just listen to what you're being told to do and try your best to do it. Third, your father doesn't like unnecessary chit-chat; it annoys him. And last, keep your spaces in the house neat and clean." Lemar re-ran the house rules in his mind. No chit-chat? I can't talk to my father. Lemar was troubled by the third rule. He loved the idle chatter with his mother, but now he was warned against being too talkative with his father, I want my mother! Lemar mumbled under his breath.

"Royce, can I ask you something," Lemar said one night just before bed.

"What's up, little cuz?" Royce replied.

"Why is my dad always so serious?" Lemar asked. He'd been around his father all his life but hadn't realized just how serious and stoic he always was. He was almost the opposite of his bubbly, friendly, energetic, and yet at times strict mother.

Royce casually answered, "Well, that's just how he is. He works hard, and he just doesn't like any nonsense from children."

"I'm afraid of him," Lemar admitted. He had never felt this way about his father before, but now that he was with him all the time, he began to see him in a different light.

"No, no, little Cuz. You Don't have to feel afraid. He's your father, and he loves you." Royce attempted to calm Lemar's fears.

"He's too serious! I feel like I'm in a camp for soldiers." Lemar mused. "I never know when it's a good time to talk, laugh, play, or anything. I feel like it's a game of Russian roulette with him."

Royce laughed, "That's funny, Cuz. Don't think too much into it. You'll be fine. Now get some sleep."

Laid up for a while at bedtime, Lemar thought about when he would see his mother next. *I can't wait for the summer so I can go see my mother.*

The next two years flew by quickly. Lemar visited his mother each summer and enjoyed the time he spent with her. They shopped on the weekends, he ate as much as he wanted, he watched television all day and then played outside with the neighbor's kids in the evening. He wished he could stay with her, but realized it simply wasn't that time yet. Lemar grew increasingly frustrated with his father and the lack of time and attention he received at home. He tried explaining this to his mother while visiting, but she said it couldn't be as bad as he said it was. But Viola knew what Lemar was dealing with, deep down inside she understood Lemar's plight; stoicism was actually one of the reasons she and Earl's relationship had failed. However, she did her best to keep Lemar positive and encouraged because she knew she didn't have an option for him to stay with her at the present time.

Lemar's frustration, however, began to take a toll on his grades; he had broken one of Earl's cardinal rules! When Lemar saw his report card, he was terrified to show it to his father. And as expected, when Earl saw the report card, he declared sternly to Lemar, "If these grades Don't improve, you're not traveling to visit your mother, or your uncle come next summer."

That threat was enough to set Lemar back on the straight and narrow, his grades improved; he was even given a certificate for being the most improved student at school.

That summer, Lemar got to visit his mother Viola and her brother Uncle Fred, in Florida. Lemar was thrilled to see his uncle and his cousins. He always enjoyed visiting them. He and his cousins were close in age; they always had barrels of fun and they entertained each other whenever they were together. Uncle Fred was the opposite of Earl. He was easy to talk to; he hung out with his sons and included Lemar. I wish my father would hang out with me. I wish he would let me relax a little. Lemar would occasionally slip away deep in thought, time after time.

One day while deep in thought, Uncle Fred suddenly asked, "Lemar, what's happening? Are you okay?"

Startled a bit, Lemar composed himself and said, "No. Not really."

"Well, tell me what's going on." He urged.

"Uncle Fred, my father is so serious all the time, and he's very strict. I Don't feel like I can really talk around him; it's making me afraid of him." Lemar confessed sadly to his uncle.

Uncle Fred had known Earl for a very long time. Since their high school days, they have been great friends. Even after the marital troubles grew between Viola and Earl, Fred and Earl still remained friends. Fred knew Earl's personality; he understood how Mr. Stoic Earl could be mistaken for militant by his son Lemar.

"Lemar, I know your father. He would never hurt you. Yes, he's very serious and stern, but he means you well." Fred encouraged Lemar. "I'll tell you what. I'll talk with your father. Is that good with you?"

"Yes. Please Uncle Fred. Thanks." Lemar replied, immediately following Uncle Fred's prompt to run off and jump into the pool with his cousins. Lemar felt the weight of the world lifted off his shoulders.

At the end of summer when Lemar arrived home, Earl sat down with him and told him he'd spoken with his uncle Fred. Earl summed up his response in two words, "Alright, Lem." Lemar thought to himself quietly, *Okay. Dad got the Message, I hope?*

The next few years were smoother between Earl and Lemar. Earl allowed Lemar some leeway with his conversations, and Lemar kept his grades up. Lemar asked Earl's permission to take even more extra lessons for school. The school was competitive, and Lemar was down for competing. Earl's finances also afforded them a new house, so now Lemar and Royce would have their own rooms. This was perfect for Royce, who could now have his girlfriends visit him in his own space away from his sometimes-annoying younger cousin/brother.

One day after school, Lemar came home and was surprised to find that his father was home early from work. Lemar greeted his dad, changed out of his school clothes and ate before getting to his homework. Earl had been reading through some paperwork and quickly scribbled his signature on a few of the pages before heading off to his room. Earl left the paperwork on the nightstand in his room, exposed so Lemar could see it (and read it) if he became curious enough. Earl told Lemar he was going out for a drive; he would be back shortly.

"Ok, dad," Lemar said, meanwhile chomping at the bit to read the papers left on the table in his dad's room. The second page was titled in bold letters, DECREE OF DIVORCE. Lemar's jaw dropped. He knew his parents lived in different countries and lived separate lives, but seeing those words brought out a new level of sadness and emotions in Lemar. Lemar reflected about his family, Wow! It's over. It's really over.

CHAPTER 33

FLY BIRDIE FLY

Celine and Charlston's plan worked like a charm. He spent an entire year courting Meshel before she agreed to go on a date with him. He was handsome, smart, and charming, young Meshel was intrigued by his intelligence. However, she was often curious as to why he never traveled. Whenever she asked him about it, he would make the excuse that he just didn't have the time due to work. Meshel didn't think much of it. She also didn't consider how it would impact her life in years to come.

Meshel and Charlston dated for a short time before he asked her to marry him. She was mildly afraid of being a wife but still somewhat willing to try. However, for the first time since her father died, she felt she would be safe in Charlston's arms and in his home. Charlston was infatuated with Meshel; it could in fact be described as an obsession. He loved her beauty, her wit, her compassionate nature, and the way she leaned on him for his strength. Meshel was enamored with the attention Charlston showered on her, while he observed her every move.

A year after she and Charlston were married, Meshel gave birth to their son, Marcus. He was their world and joy. Marcus was very handsome; he was indeed blessed with good looks from both of his parents. Charlston, Meshel, and Marcus appeared to be the quintessential family unit as they openly did everything together. However, despite what most of their family and friends viewed as a blessing, Meshel often felt it was a moderate curse.

Over the years, the things that made Meshel love Charleston

were also the same things that made her dislike him. What she once loved about all the attention he gave her had now begun to feel like obsession and control. The difference in their ages began to manifest in the things Meshel enjoyed or hated doing. Charlston was just the homely type; besides the sporadic local vacations or occasional trips to visit family and friends within the island country, Charlston preferred to be home taking care of his property. Meshel, on the other hand, desired to travel more and spend more time out, even overseas. She began to feel like she was suffocating. The father figure she found in her husband was now the image of a man she resented.

One evening, during one of Charlston's call to his aunt in the United States, Meshel overheard Charlston arguing with her. Her voice pierced the air around the phone, "Charlston, you have no patience for marriage and children!" Needless to say, Meshel was curious about his aunt's comment, but she hesitated and then procrastinated to ask him about it. She did, however, take note that he didn't debate his aunt's statement. He never uttered a word of disagreement.

One day, Charlston asked Meshel if she and Marcus could join him for a visit to a friend's house. Meshel had never met this friend, but she agreed to go. From the outside when they arrived, Meshel noticed burning candles inside many windows of the house.

There were already other women and wives at the house, and

all their children played inside. Marcus was always shy around strangers, he usually stayed close to Meshel until he felt comfortable enough to venture off on his own. As they made their way into the kitchen, Marcus pointed at the window and asked, "Mommy, who is that man outside?" Meshel looked out the window, but she didn't see anyone.

"Marcus, I Don't see anyone. Maybe it was one of the kids." Meshel responded.

By this time, Meshel was annoyed with Marcus and decided to send him upstairs to the playroom where some of the kids played. When they got to the bottom of the staircase, Marcus pointed to the top of the staircase and said, "Mommy, mommy. The man at the top of the steps is not going to let me pass by."

Meshel was embarrassed and said to Marcus, with her teeth clenched, "Marcus, stop it! There's no one at the top of the stairs."

That's when Meshel heard the hostess of the party, the wife of Charlston's friend say, "No. It's okay. He's right, and that's my guardian angel he sees."

The hairs on the back of Meshel's neck, and on her forearms raised from her fear. She became frustrated with Marcus and then angry with Charlston. "WHAT?!" She faced the woman and asked. "What's going on here?"

Charlston rushed over and put his hands on Meshel's shoulders, "Calm down, Luv."

"Calm down? What is going on here? Is this some kind of witchcraft?" Meshel yelled at her husband.

Marcus was shivering and gripped his mother's hand as tight as he could. Meshel, with Marcus in tow, headed through the front door. "Get me and my son out of here now!" She demanded of Charlston.

Charlston tried to calm her down, he tried to convince her that staying was okay, but Meshel would hear none of it. "Lord have mercy. Charlston, we are leaving here now!"

Charlston had stayed in the kitchen talking with his friend, so he didn't witness everything that took place, he couldn't understand why Meshel was so upset. He apologized to his friend and the rest of their guests before joining Meshel outside.

"Did you know about this, Charleston?" Meshel asked.

"About what, Meshel?" He retorted.

As they got into his car, Meshel slammed the door as quickly as she could. She turned to Charlston, proceeded to tell him what happened with Marcus at the steps, and asked about all the candles in the windows. "What about your friend's wife saying it was her guardian angel? She's an adult. You Don't think that's strange for a grown person to say?" Marcus pushed his head into her chest as she recounted the event.

"Meshel, stop talking foolishness. That never happened!"

Charlston said, attempting to debunk her account of everything.

Meshel became furious at Charlston's disbelief and insisted, "Yes, it did! Why would I make that up? Look at your son. He's scared to death." Meshel lifted Marcus' head from her chest so Charlston could see the fear in his eyes. "Why would you have us come to these people's house when you know they're into this weird mess? I can't believe you would do this to me and your son. Tell me something, are you into this stuff as well?"

A sudden calm overshadowed Charlston as he replied, "It's not that serious, Meshel."

Meshel was incensed that her husband didn't seem to take the situation as seriously as she did. She began to believe he was into those same types of beliefs. *Oh, really? Not that serious, eh? He must be into this weird stuff too. Is this why he never wants to travel abroad?* But Meshel kept her thoughts to herself.

After that incident, Meshel felt a bit insecure. She somehow convinced Charlston to let Pamela stay with them for a while. The house was big enough, and there was plenty of room. With Pamela around, Meshel's mind was more at ease. However, Charlston grew tired of their house guest because Pamela's presence began to interfere with his time with Meshel.

Meshel preferred to spend late nights gossiping and laughing with Pamela. Charlston would ask, "Meshel, are you coming to bed soon?"

Meshel and Pamela giggled as Meshel responded, "Yes. I'm coming soon," knowing she didn't have any plans of going to bed anytime soon. Meshel had grown tired of Charlston and confided in Pamela. She felt trapped. She wanted to enjoy more time with her sister and be free to travel abroad. Meshel's attraction toward Charlston was quickly fading. Her curiosity for the outside world was genuinely renewed, and she yearned for more excitement.

Charlston was desperate to keep Meshel tied to their marriage. He was willing to try just about anything to preserve their relationship. Meshel naivety to Charlston's dark beliefs was fading quickly. He had successfully hidden his practices until one day, she discovered a sheet of paper in one of his dresser drawers with her and Pamela's names written on it about a hundred times. There was black thread and a needle wrapped in the paper. The findings startled Meshel. She confided in Pamela about what she found. They both agreed that it was weird, and Meshel needed to find a way to get herself and Marcus away from him.

CHAPTER 34

SWIMMING IN TRUST

Lemar made many attempts before he finally learned to swim. After many years and almost drowning twice, he eventually taught himself to swim during one summer holiday while on vacation with his dad Earl. Earl was happy for his son, but he would have been even happier if Lemar had trusted him enough to have actually learned to swim when he tried to teach him all those times when he was younger. Lemar got the hang of it, there was a new world for him in the waters.

Lemar's uncle Vee and cousin Royce moved into sections of Earl's large house he mortgaged in the city suburbs; effectively, Earl, Vee, Royce, and Lemar now spent more time together in one home. Sunday afternoons in Jamaica were the traditional big day for the average man and his family or girlfriend to go swimming. Whether in warm sandy crystal beach waters, or in the chilly free-flowing river currents hidden between the gaps of mountains and hills, both scenes were surrounded by their own types of greenery including the popular coconut trees. The beaches were supplied with fresh wild salty snapper fish, lionfish and jewfish; the rivers filled with freshwater options like perch, killifish and gobies. Men and boys splash the waters to release stress and swim to exhibit their 'acquired' aquatic skills, all before the duties and blues and rush-hour traffic again come Monday morning for work and school.

Lemar would always travel to swim with his dad Earl, while Royce would ride along with Uncle Vee. Vee was less enthusiastic about swimming, so Royce sometimes joined Earl and Lemar, or sometimes would tag along much later with his own friends. The journey to the beach was a two-hour drive along the causeways, then through sandy windswept roads to find the perfect parking spot. Earl preferred to leave early on Sunday mornings while the sky was still dark, just so he could observe the glorious bright sunrise as he drove; he also beat the crowd and enjoyed first dibs at an uncluttered beach. Both he and Vee knew where to park so they could meet each other once they arrived.

Lemar felt secure swimming with his dad because Earl was a very strong swimmer. Once Uncle Vee, Cousin Royce, and Royce's friends arrived, he felt even more safe and protected. Earl could swim in deeper waters for longer periods than Lemar could handle. Usually, Lemar would trail Earl as far as he possibly could, but invariably Earl would leave him behind after a short while and keep going until he was almost a speck in the water to Lemar's view of him. Lemar was never rude to his father about leaving him behind, only saddened by his inability to compete with the man of the house at this activity. Eventually, Earl would pop up on Lemar in the water to show his presence, giving him a feeling of camaraderie again.

One Sunday, Lemar was excited as he anticipated putting on the diver's mask, he found floating near the beach shoreline a couple of weeks prior. He ventured out into the water, wading around in the shallow clear blue salty sea, then he swam further out. Lemar's feet could no longer touch the bottom, so he had to tread water or swim to stay afloat. He was enjoying the sight of the sand, seaweed, and occasional Crayola-colors of fish swimming around him. He was quickened to keep up with his dad, Earl had swam further offshore.

Lemar immersed his head under the water and, thanks to his diver's mask, could see the fluffy white splashes of his dad's feet. He was fascinated by the sea life swirling around him, darting about, and living freely in their habitat. Lemar was so focused on the wildlife that he lost sight of his dad. He lifted his head above the water to see if he spotted his dad, but Earl was nowhere in sight. Then suddenly, three bluish-green snake-like creatures shot out from beneath Lemar.

Panic began to set in, and Lemar's arms and legs began to feel like weights. He seemed to have forgotten how to maneuver in the water and quickly sank under. He flailed his arms and legs wildly. *Oh, man! Where's Dad? Am I going to drown?* Lemar dreaded, as he went back under the water, he began coordinating his arms and legs and felt his body propelling forward and upwards. He swam for what felt like hours into the shallow water. He could see the sand bed rising towards his feet, planted his feet, and stood up straight in the water. He spun his body around, still searching for the sight of his dad. Where is he? Fear gripped Lemar as he worried that something might have happened to his father in the water.

As he lifted the mask from his face, he looked towards the shoreline and eyed a brown dog barking in his direction. A few feet away, Lemar saw a strong lean body waving both hands at him. *Is that Dad?* Lemar asked himself, wiping away the water cascading down his face, mask now off so he could see clearly. His dad was standing there, waving for Lemar to come out of the water. Lemar was embarrassed that the beach full of onlookers had sat and watched him panic in the water and furious that his dad was acting so nonchalantly as he walked out of the tides and surf towards him.

As he got closer to Earl, Lemar put the mask back on his forehead to hide the look of disgust on his face. How could he leave me alone in the water? "Dad, did you see those three snakes in the water? Lemar asked.

"Yes. I saw them. They weren't snakes, they were eels. They are dangerous! That's why I came out of the water." Earl responded.

Lemar stood there, shocked at his dad's response. *That's why you came out of the water, and so fast too?* Lemar thought about it, but didn't ask the question; why did you leave me out there? Disappointed in his father, he didn't understand why he didn't forewarn him of the danger, besides leaving him behind. For the greater part of that afternoon, Lemar was quiet. He didn't say much until he saw his uncle Vee and Royce walking towards Earl and himself from afar. Lemar thought, *I can't wait to tell Uncle Vee and Royce about this.*

Lemar's trust and respect for his dad faded that day. Uncle Vee spoke with Earl about the incident afterward, but Earl wasn't convinced he had done anything wrong. "He's growing up, and he knows how to swim," was Earl's response. Lemar forgave his father and maintained his respect for him, but he never forgot how he abandoned him at such a critical moment of time.

CHAPTER 35

DISCOVERING

THE ROAD

Over the years, Meshel developed a great relationship with Charlston's aunt Thea. They would spend countless hours on the phone talking about "lady things," as Charlston often referred to their long talks. Thea finally convinced Meshel to bring Marcus to the United States to visit her and the rest of the family. Initially, Charlston was hesitant to agree to Marcus and Meshel traveling alone out of the country, since she had never traveled abroad before. However, once Meshel's younger brother, Roland, decided to travel with them, Charlston agreed. Roland and Charlston shared a special bond as Charlston became a mentor to the young Roland who expressed an interest in becoming a businessman. Roland also shared a unique connection with Charlston's aunt, who was a fantastic cook; she spent a lot of time teaching Roland her culinary acumen. Their relationship expanded the trust Charlston had in his young brother-in-law.

Aunt Thea lived near Waterbury, Connecticut. Both Meshel and Roland were amazed at how much It felt like the wild open country; very few buses and cars, lots of farmland, and big country houses. It wasn't anything like the cityscape they envisioned. They expected crowds of people bustling about busy streets while cars honked their horns, trying to escape gridlock traffic. They were ready to be part of the action. They hoped to indulge in the fast-paced and stimulating American city life they'd heard about over the years. But they were quickly disappointed by the slow-paced, quiet, and yes, dull albeit beautiful landscape they encountered surrounding aunt Thea's house. Little Marcus, on the other hand, was in a dream world. There was cable TV with so many channels for him to watch. He enjoyed the fresh air and running about the 1-acre open field that was Aunt Thea's yard. He chased grasshoppers through the beautiful botanicals in Thea's garden and tried catching lightning bugs in small mason jars when they began to glow at sunset.

There was a constant flow of family members visiting Meshel, Marcus, and Roland at Thea's house. Food was plentiful, and love was abundant. Marcus met many of his cousins, and he enjoyed all the attention and the many playmates his age. Meshel loved seeing her son so happy. She would feel a knot develop in the pit of her belly every time she thought about taking him back home at the end of their visit.

Roland was in his own dream world. The women flocked to him at every turn. They were mesmerized by his long-braided dread-locs. They offered him meals, invited him out, and vied for his attention. Thea would say, "Look at these women falling all over themselves for the attention of this handsome young man." They'd all crack up laughing. Roland was a gentleman but still somewhat naïve, adding to his charisma and charm. Meshel saw how happy her brother was and wished he could stay in the United States. She found herself wanting to stay as well. She cringed at the thought of going home and living under Charlston's thumb. However, she really missed Pamela, she missed her immensely.

Meshel recalled her aunt Kay telling her that she had some family in the states who happened to also live in Connecticut. One afternoon, Thea agreed to drive Meshel and Roland to spend the weekend with their cousin, Anette. The drive was scenic, and they could experience a small portion of the city life as they sat in Friday afternoon gridlocked traffic on Interstate 95. But Thea was a patient driver. She and Roland talked and laughed the entire ride while Meshel drifted in and out of deep thought. *I have to find a way for us to stay. Roland and Marcus are so happy. We just can't go back to stay. We just can't!*

Anette was taken by Meshel's beauty and just how much she and Roland resembled her uncle David. Anette was stunning as well. She and Meshel could pass for sisters. She was excited to have Meshel and Roland over and couldn't wait to take them out to meet her friends. They hugged Thea and said their see-you-laters' before dropping their bags in Anette's guest room. They spent most of the day and early evening listening to stories about their father's childhood and other family stories. Their aunts, uncles, and cousins spilled into the house one by one. Meshel and Roland were overwhelmed with all the love they received from Charlston's family and now their very own. They'd wished that Estelle, Roger, Pamela, and their other brothers and sisters could be there.

Later that evening, once the house was empty of most of the family and the others were off to bed, or their regular nightly routines, Anette, Meshel, Roland, and a few other cousins got dressed to go to one of the local nightclubs. Meshel and Roland were ecstatic to be partying in the states. They were finally enjoying the lifestyle they'd heard so much about. The music was loud; there was barely elbow room as the club was jammed-packed. Roland was immediately swept onto the dance floor by an eager young woman admiring his braided locs, handsome face, and well-built body. Meshel laughed as Roland looked back with a wide grin on his face.

Anette and Meshel headed to the bar, where they ordered drinks. They managed to make their way through the crowd despite being bumped along the way. They ignored all the advances made by the admiring men. One young man waved them over to take a seat on the black leather lounge bench in the VIP section. He greeted them and said, "You beautiful ladies can sit here in my section." They thanked him and took their seats.

Meshel and Anette motioned their bodies to the beat of the music blasting through the sound system. They watched Roland grind with different women who were desperate to rub up against him. Their cups were replaced before they could finish their drinks as the server abided by the orders of the young man to "take care of them." As the night grew later, Meshel and Anette were ready to head back to the house. Roland was caught up with one young lady in whom he seemed to be thoroughly interested. He assured them he was "okay" and that he'd meet them back at the house. The young lady confirmed that she would "drive him home." They smiled and headed for the door when Meshel felt someone gently grab her hand.

"Where are you going, pretty lady?" the young man asked.

Meshel smiled at the familiar face of the gentleman who made sure she and Anette were comfortable all night. "It's late. We are headed home."

He smiled at Meshel's silky accent, "So, were you just going to leave without telling me your name?"

"Oh! Sorry to be rude. My name is Meshel." She responded. "Well, Meshel, did you enjoy yourself? He asked.

"I did. I had a great time." Meshel smiled as she answered. "You have such a beautiful smile." He said, flirting.

Anette interjected, "Don't you think you should tell her your name?"

"Oh, sorry. Yes, my name is Asher," he shared.

Anette continued, tickled by the young man's almost child-like flirting with Meshel, "Don't you think you should give her your number so she can call you tomorrow?

Meshel was stunned by Anette's directness. She admired her cousin's boldness; it reminded her of herself. Asher wrote his phone number on a piece of paper and handed it to Meshel.

"I hope to hear from you tomorrow," he said.

"You will," Anette answered for Meshel.

Meshel jokingly rolled her eyes at her cousin, turned to Asher, and said, "You will."

Meshel was now determined that she had to return to the United States.

CHAPTER 36

TRAIN TO THE GAME

The NFL game started at 9 pm. If Lemar left the City College's computer lab by 7:15 pm, he would catch the subway train and get home in time to watch the New York Giants kickoff at 9 pm.

Lemar was hardly focused. He was distracted as he plodded through the coding language onscreen for his introductory programming computer class homework. The Giants were on the edge of playing for the NFC championship, and Lawrence Taylor was wreaking havoc against opposing quarterbacks. On this Monday night, football was going to be his priority. The ever-present yet unreliable New York City subway was the only factor between Lemar and the game. He lived at the last stop but hoped to get the express train to get home quicker.

Dressing real preppie in a sweater, the latest Jordan sneakers, and blue jeans, Lemar looked clean cut for the ladies, especially if those ladies rode in the last of the ten cabs of every subway train. Riding in the last cab was always exciting and drama filled. Fights, robberies, undercover police pulling people off the train, subway dance crews, boom-box radios playing hip-hop, the latest fashions and footwear, hot girls, all kinds of girls, beggars, junkies, religious preachers, political activism. The list goes on and on. Lemar inhaled it all, including the secondhand Kush smoke, which was lightweight compared to the raw bush-weed smoke he encountered growing up in Jamaica. It was common sense that he should avoid the last car of the train, but he was not afraid. If all else failed, he could run very fast.

Activating the air brakes on the subway was meant to be for emergency stops only! Too often, someone would get into one of the subway conductor's booths and pull the emergency air brakes. Lemar's twenty-five to thirty-five-minute ride tonight would take two hours instead.

It was 7:35 PM when he boarded the train; the ride was initially not so bad, with very few delays. The train was just half-way into the East Tremont Avenue station of the Bronx when he heard the infamous air brakes go SWOOSH!!! *C'mon, man, not again, not now. I Don't need another delay*, thought Lemar while steaming from his ears.

Lemar looked at his watch, and it was already 8:06 pm. Less than an hour before the game starts, I can still make the kick-off. Anxiety had him exhaling, releasing some of his annoyance like extra steam. He thought, *Time check again.* It was 8:16 pm. The second half of the train was still outside of the station, and the entire train now hovered twenty-five feet above the hustling-busy-steamy Bronx streets below. The smoke from the manholes rose past the train windows. In the cold of the night, the smoke looked like the breath of a giant's nostrils. *Speaking of Giants, I'm going to miss this NY Giants game tonight!* He thought.

As the time slipped away, he sat in the last car, looking ahead though the side window at the station. People waited for the train to pull in completely so they could enter and exit. The second cab ahead of his cab was packed like sardines with people! These were the smart people. They preferred to squeeze together instead of facing the drama in the last cab, ignoring that there was guaranteed personal space to stretch their legs in moderate comfort and urban street style.

This really sucks! he thought; maybe I can get home right after the kickoff? He thought further, trying to console himself.

He didn't do a head count but, while sitting back, took a nonchalant scan to his left and then to his right. He saw that the train cab was practically empty, with very few people.

Lemar closed his eyes and clenched his teeth in frustration for a brief minute; it seemed time moved quickly with every blink of his eye. It was now 8:54 pm, and he realized he couldn't catch the football game's beginning. He gives up, letting out a sigh. He opens his eyes and turns his head to look toward the front of the cab. There is movement between the second and last cabs. It looks…, it looks like the police!

It was mid-November, so it was cold and already nighttime. The officers were clearly in a huddle, discussing their game plan. The silence is broken, as everyone in the cab looks at the door when one of the officers enters, he has a darker chocolate complexion than Lemar. The officer looked at everyone in the subway cab, his hands remained in the pockets of his uniform. He walks past each person. Lemar was the third of five people in the car; the second person, clearly an older man, clearly a retiree.

The officer passes everyone almost twice, then posts his back against the subway doors opposite Lemar, his hands never leaving his pockets. Everyone in the cab remains as silent as mice.

The noisy door again, and in walks a second officer, the first officer, was simply a distraction for his partner to enter in unexpectedly. This second officer was clearly Latino, lighter complexioned, hands also in his pockets; he headed straight to an open space right next to Lemar's seat. Lemar sits up straight, looking at both of the officers in his presence. What's going on here? He thought nervously.

This was late fall of 1989. Between the police, folks about street-life, and ordinary regular jaded New York City slickers, the tension was high. Spike Lee's film "Do The Right Thing" was released before the summer of the same year, so the streets were on edge. The New York City mayor struggled to calm the stress. The outgoing police commissioner locked horns with the mayor too many times publicly, then the commissioner left for a college teaching job in his hometown to be with his family.

New York City, at the time, employed over 29,000 police officers, the largest single police force in the nation. Residency was a key issue; officers should be residents of the areas they patrolled. Hence, they would be better able to interpret and handle situations, de-escalate situations, and not unnecessarily overreact to some situations.

While Lemar's thoughts flashed through the climate of the

times, unexpectedly a third police officer walks into the subway cab. This officer, however, has his 'midnight black .38 special' revolver in hand, trigger cocked, pointed to the floor, ready for action! Lemar took another head count, *one - two - three - four - five, including me*! He felt pressure in his head as his temples started to thump. *SOMEBODY'S ABOUT TO GET SHOT!*

The officer had his hat pulled tightly over his eyes. He looks at each passenger as he walks past everyone, including his partners. He turns, rather abruptly, at the end of the cab and walks back towards Lemar. Lemar was already clutching his bookbag, ready to leave, wanting to avoid any shrapnel or danger from the gunplay itching to take place at any moment. Unfortunately for Lemar, he was their target!

The third officer walks up to and points the gun directly at Lemar's head. Then, like the main character in the movie Robocop, the officer said, "STEP FORWARD WITH YOUR HANDS UP!" Lemar did not feel any fear, he felt insulted, and he was very angry at the officer pointing the gun at him for no reason. Lemar looked down the dark tunnel of the barrel of the officer's gun; the gun was less than twelve inches from his face. From his seat he looked upwards, directly into the officer's eyes, he had a clear view of the officer's eyes tucked under his tightly pulled black police hat. Foolishly, though bravely, Lemar refuses to budge at the officer's command; instead, he firmly and resonantly requests that the officer explains, "FOR WHAT?"

The second officer, standing immediately next to Lemar, blasted the next command, "JUST DO IT!"

Lemar, still highly annoyed at the officers, doesn't budge. He looks at the first officer standing across the train aisle facing him. There was no pity in his eyes for Lemar. *What did I do?* Lemar began to ask himself. *I know I didn't do anything to deserve this!*

Lemar stands straight up like a soldier at attention, popping up from his bench seat. His bookbag still hung high on his shoulder. He did not want to fight the police, but he was ready to do it. Courage under fear leapt into his entire being, but it was controlled courage, not wild, unrestrained courage. At this moment, Lemar still felt no fear.

Another person enters the subway cab. Lemar saw the movement but was preoccupied with Mr. Robocop pointing the gun in his face. It was a young man just like himself in age and complexion. He paused, looked at Lemar in bewilderment, and then cried out, "IT WASN'T HIM!!!"

Lemar was still upset, he looked at the young man and said, "Were you going to wait until I was shot before you opened your mouth?" There was silence…, then the young man cried again to the officers, "It wasn't him." There was a private huddle between all three officers and the young man. Despite their apparent attempts to whisper, Lemar overheard enough bits and pieces, thus realizing that the young man had been robbed of his wallet by another young man just like himself, as soon as the train left the previous station. Apparently, the robber was also well dressed, quite similar to Lemar's outfit, and in similar colors. *These clothes I'm wearing almost cost me my life*, Lemar thought.

Officer number three, still with his revolver cocked, is shocked as he gets clarity from the young man. He uncocks the hammer of his pistol, keeping it pointed toward the floor, he spins about-face like a robotic ballerina, and heads toward the back of the subway car to further interrogate the last passenger, another young man just like Lemar and the robbery victim. While tugging at the young man's pants pockets and coat, it was evident to everyone on the train that this was a search without merit, so he eventually stopped, as the agitated young man repeatedly asked, "Yo! Why are you doing this?"

The young man who was robbed, feels ashamed as he watches officer number three's unjustifiable frisk-and-search of the other young man, so he leaves the cab along with the first two officers. These two officers adjusted the collars of their uniforms and fixed their hats on their way out as they realized how close they came to executing another young New York male over a mistaken identity. They make their way out and ease their way through the passengers of the next crowded subway cab, heading toward the front of the train.

Lemar sits back down, his bookbag still draped on his tensed shoulder. Officer number three is left alone by his partners, but finally puts his gun away in its holster. He begins his lonely walk of shame and tips his hat off his eyes as he passes Lemar. He looked briefly at Lemar and said, "Thank you for your cooperation!"

Co-operation? Lemar's anger thumped in his head again. What f***ing co-operation? You put a gun to my head for no reason and talk about cooperation. Not thinking rationally, the lion of rage rises in Lemar once again. He looks into the eyes of officer number three, but the officer breaks eye contact immediately and turns his head to walk on. "F^@% YOU!!! YOU PUT A GUN TO MY HEAD AND TALK ABOUT COOPERATION, F^@% YOU!!!" Were Lemar's words as officer three departed through the same door as his partners. Officer three really had to adjust his collar, he almost took his hat off as he appeared to be sweating, suddenly the top of his uniform collar looked wet from sweat. He was nervous.

Officer number three chose to spare Lemar, he kept his hand away from his revolver. Though nervous, he shrugs off Lemar's outburst; he ignores Lemar as he thinks of what to do, versus what could have just happened. He could have killed another mother's child with indiscretion.

There was still a delay in getting the train cleared for movement by the officers. Lemar has now lost his appetite for watching the NFL football game, and of course he also lost his desire to continue riding in the last cab of the subway train. As he emerges into the second cab, Lemar squeezes past a few passengers who are all staring at him.

"Are you okay?" Lemar looked up, it was the voice of an older lady. She could have easily been his mother. He replied politely, "Yes. I'm okay, thanks."

"Young brother, can I speak with you for a minute?" Halfway through the second cab, Lemar now looked back, scanning the passengers he just squeezed by, searching for the face of the man with the resonant raspy voice who beckoned his attention from amongst the crowd. The man raises his hand, identifying himself to Lemar. Lemar squeezes past the passengers again and stands next to the man. The man's name is Matthew Jones.

CHAPTER 37

THE LECTERN

Mr. Jones is an educator, a teacher, and a preacher. He looks at Lemar, evaluating him through the lens of his steel-framed eyeglasses.

"Yes, sir." Lemar greets the older man.

Mr. Jones begins his speech to Lemar, "Young man, we saw and heard what happened with you and the police just now. First, I want to commend you on your bravery. However, I also want to caution you about riding in the last cab of these subway trains. You seem to be a well-mannered, intelligent person, but now do you see why we choose to pack ourselves like sardines in this cab and not ride in that last subway cab?

Lemar felt pressured, standing in the midst of everyone in the cab. "I do, sir." He said.

"You could have lost your life just now, not because you are a part of the criminal element in these streets of New York, but because you chose to dwell among the entities that profess themselves to be smarter than the reach of the law and the reach of the Lord's hands." Mr. Jones pauses to observe Lemar's facial expressions as the rest of the passengers listen keenly to his lecture.

Clearly, this man chooses his words differently from most people I've listened to, including my professors, Lemar thought. "I know better, but I get to sit comfortably."

"Well, you seem to be quite able-bodied and able to handle yourself. What is the problem with associating yourself with the smarter element and putting yourself at a lower risk of harm by taking a stance in this subway cab or the other subway cabs so you can get home safely? The older people here deal with the stress for just a short space of time, and then they can leave this sardine, tin-can, environment to get home safely."

Lemar was amused by his lecturer's speech patterns, but at the same time, he felt mocked and chastised by the warnings coming from this stranger. Lemar responded, "I'll take that into consideration next time, sir."

The stranger is impressed with Lemar's manners, as a matter of fact, he is astonished at Lemar's poise in his responses.

"Young man, I see a strong presence with you. We need young men like yourself to step up and be examples to our people, not to be statistics of disorder for other people to gossip about. I do preach the word. Do you know what that means?" He asks Lemar.

"You preach the Bible?" Lemar asked.

"That is correct, and I have also lectured on history at some of our universities. Let me offer you my card and my services. Perhaps one day you can become of service to our people. By the way, my name is Matthew Jones."

Lemar took the card from Mr. Jones and looked carefully at his credentials.

After that incident, Lemar better understood the phrase 'as

courageous as a lion.' The response of an individual under the fear of real threats of pressure and danger. He ponders the lecture of Mr. Jones, his prior knowledge of bad choices, then reaffirms to himself, I'm not riding in the last subway cab just for the fun of it anymore.

Finally, Lemar gets home. The NFL game was already near the end of the first quarter. The Giants won the game; but weeks later, they lost the NFC East Division title game to the Los Angeles Rams. Lemar never told his family what happened on the subway train. He already knew what he did wrong, he didn't want another lecture, but he was and remains truly grateful for the lecture he got from Mr. Jones.

Many years after this horrific experience, Lemar would drive his vehicle through the same streets he once walked on or traveled through on subway trains, observing at times the same trains rumbling along overhead and police officers on patrol in cars or on foot, surveying the neighborhoods. There were times when Lemar had to stop his vehicle for police spot checks. Lemar always looked the officer at his window in the eyes as he answered the questions asked. He always made it a point to thank them for their public service, then they always bid him "Have a good day sir." He respected their role in society, he never prejudiced his view of the police officers as all bad.

After this horrific experience, Lemar still always respected the authority of police officers and even had childhood friends and new friends that were police officers and detectives. The moral of the story was to not judge all police by the behavior of the bad officers. There are good cops, and then there are bad cops.

CHAPTER 38

ROAD THROUGH RHONDA

Meshel struggled to gain her footing while staying with Roland and his new girlfriend in the United States. She didn't have many skills to apply for most of the available jobs. Most of her skills were attributed to caregiving, so she decided to pursue employment that would allow her to be a caregiver. One afternoon while browsing through social media, Meshel stumbled across a post from a familiar face. Is that Rhonda? She's here, in the states? She sent a friend request to Rhonda. A few minutes after her invitation, Rhonda accepted the request. Meshel was excited and took to scrolling through Rhonda's profile and pictures. She noticed that Rhonda also lived in Connecticut, not too far from Thea. She also noticed that Rhonda had four children—three daughters and a son. They were all adorned in the latest urban fashion and appeared very happy.

Meshel wasted no time reaching out to Rhonda. She sent a message,

"Hi, Rhonda. I remember you from school back home. How have you been?"

"Hi Meshel, How have you been?"

"Fine, thank you. I have two kids now. Are those pretty young girls and the handsome little boy all yours?"

"That's good, Meshel. Yes, they are all my children. I would love to meet up with you if you are in town?"

"Sure. Here's my number. 555-225-3434"

"Got it! My number is 555-345-1910."

Meshel called Rhonda the next day. Rhonda's demeanor hadn't changed much since the last time Meshel saw her. She was still a bully, and there was a coldness and ignorance about her vernacular.

"I'm looking for a job. Do you know anyone looking to hire a caregiver?" Meshel asked Rhonda.

"Girl, I Don't know about any jobs right now, but you can call my Aunt Rose. Take her number. She might know of something," answered Rhonda matter-of-factly.

Meshel called Rhonda's aunt and explained why Rhonda had shared her number.

"I'm looking for a job. I'm trying to get my finances together so I can find my own place and bring my boys home with me." Meshel shared.

Meshel was taken aback by the woman's harshness, "Cheese-and-crackers! Look here, girl, I Don't know about any jobs, and I Don't know why Rhonda told you to call me!"

When Meshel called Rhonda again, she sensed her annoyance when she answered the phone, "Huh-Lo!"

"Hey, Rhonda, I spoke with your aunt, but she was kind of rude and ran me off the phone," Meshel said.

Rhonda wasn't moved by Meshel's account. Her aunt had already called her and given her a piece of her mind, and she didn't care to talk about it any further.

Rhonda replied, "Well, right now, I Don't know about any jobs, girl. I can't help you right now!" She hung up the phone.

Meshel continued her job search with no luck. Roland encouraged her to keep at it. He assured her she could stay as long as needed until she got herself together. He was sure to cover her cell phone bill so she could communicate with potential employers. A few weeks had gone by since Meshel spoke to Rhonda, until one day, her phone rang, and she was surprised to hear Rhonda's voice on the other end.

"Meshel! Girl! Get a pen and a piece of paper. Write this down." Rhonda got straight to the point.

"Hi, Rhonda. Okay." Meshel grabbed a pen and pad.

"The man of the house takes three sugars in his tea, and the wife takes the blue pills at night. I'll text you the directions to the place. The work is easy, and the pay is good. Don't call me to ask any questions, eh! You wrote it down already?" Rhonda's sentences rushed one into the next.

"Yes," Meshel answered.

"Good! This is my weekend off. Don't call me back, eh!" Rhonda hung up the phone before Meshel could thank her.

Meshel jumped to her feet and cried out, "I GOT A JOB!"

CHAPTER 39

LEARNING THE ROPES

Lemar was not a teenager anymore, he was now in his early twenties, and he came to the conclusion that life is about making choices, sometimes those choices meant sacrificing one thing for another and that included sacrificing bad friendships to make things good. He struggled with losing friendships, being a loyal person was his natural way of thinking. Timing in life was another lesson learned through his father Earl who enforced promptness, along with a tough-through-it mentality, where he pursued and obtained the things he wanted, as his own brainchild. However, Lemar would have to adjust his mindset as he explored the world he knew, settling and compromising for harmonious relationships, while focusing and elevating towards his goals, in his pursuit of happiness.

While he preferred working alone or hustling alone, he began to realize that having at least one trustworthy partner was essential for building the financial success he desired. He often heard the quote, "No man is an island," but was he ready to open himself up to finding that first trustworthy and dependable partner? He fought himself on being too secretive and cagy with people, he was playing it cool and trusted the process more than he fought the flow of events. It was lukewarm excitement for Lemar.

The opposing thoughts in his mind fought like two boxers for the championship of controlling his final decisions. How will I know if they're the right person, that's if they are trustworthy? What if I mess up? Will they have my back? What if they overreact to petty mistakes? Lemar increasingly grappled with the dueling thoughts in his mind.

He stayed gainfully employed, kept his regular job as a technician. He was young, smart, technically savvy, ambitious, and assertive, and his bosses loved that. They had plans for Lemar's bright future in their company. However, Lemar had his own business aspirations in mind. He was naive, but determined to build a thriving business that would eventually allow him to retire early, without having to look back into the dark tunnel of regrets.

Lemar's vision of entrepreneurship was a path to his mere desire for freedom! He wanted financial independence and personal freedom; at the end of this journey, he wanted peace of mind. He began working on his empire-of-freedom one venture at a time. Armed with an array of business ideas under his hat, he drew them all out on a single piece of paper. One at a time, maybe some simultaneously, but at the end of the day he still struggled with one thing, identifying a solid long-term partner.

Lemar's first partnership was with some of his more knowledgeable friends and acquaintances, process servers who served summonses of all kinds for the courts. It certainly wasn't a part of his passion, in fact it felt like a bit of a detour from his goals, but until the money came pouring in, they assured him that the opportunity, though somewhat dangerous, would generate "good money" on the sidelines. Lemar was all in.

They advised him to get his license to serve summons from the department of consumer affairs, as well as a permit to carry firearms in the event of hostile resistance by anyone angry at receiving a summons to appear in court. Once Lemar was certified for both, he was energized. Armed with both license and permit, he bought himself a Taurus PT-25 firearm. Recommended by his oldest acquaintance Perry, he said "it's been reliable, hardly ever jam; I've had mine for some years now, it's durable; and I get good accuracy at the range. Trust me, you won't regret it. Some of the other firearms you hear about all the time are good, but this is just as good, without being a part of a popularity contest."

Lemar fell into the spell of Perry's advice and encouragement, the ownership of the weapon was less intriguing than the camaraderie he expected from joining this 'elite' crew of brave hearts. His excitement, however, didn't last long. After all his efforts, his new business partners failed to show up for the initial business meetings with the accountant they hired to help them set up their company.

But that didn't stop Lemar. He completed all the legal documents with the same accountant and set up a new company on his own. He was officially CEO and ready to move on with his next business venture.

Lemar wasn't a timid young man. After witnessing his aunt being raped and being harassed by the police at gunpoint on the train, he was relentless at chasing whatever goal he thought was worth the effort and time. Then after three weeks, one of his friends finally called him; ignoring the fact they missed the original meeting with the accountant, Lemar made his determination very clear to this 'friend,' Damon.

"Hey, Lem! You ready to go register this business?" said Damon.

"Business? I tried calling you all several times on the day we were supposed to meet with the accountant. None of you answered or got back to me!" Not you, Perry, or any of the other guys. Lemar responded. He was annoyed at the disregard of Damon's attitude.

"We had to sort through some things first, but we're ready now!" Damon eagerly answered on behalf of the crew.

"So, none of you were able to call me to tell me that?" Lemar snapped.

"We had something to handle, I said!" Damon said, pushing back at Lemar.

Lemar's frustration increased. His friend didn't seem to understand basic common courtesy. These guys are flaky. I can't count on them. If they Don't get it now, then they'll do this again in the future. Lemar pondered the friendship, the advice, the loyalty, his decision, limiting the relationship with them, pending an ending...

"Listen, I've already registered the business, and I'm going to move ahead on my own." Lemar blasted back at Damon.

"Alright, Lemar. Do your thing, peace!" At the unapologetic final words of Damon their call abruptly ended.

The business grew slowly over the next few months. It was part-time, and larger companies charged lower fees making greater profits through volumes of work handled. Lemar on his own couldn't compete and he was unwilling to partner with anyone anymore. Lemar faced reality, and remembering his true passions, he finally gave up his process server business. This was a major lesson learned. He'd lost time and money; now he trusted fewer friends, he didn't like it, but he learned to stick to his passions.

CHAPTER 40

WORKAHOLIC

Meshel worked every possible hour she could handle, trying to save enough money to get her own place and her children all under one roof. The elderly couple that Rhonda connected her with required lots of help, which allowed Meshel to accumulate as many working hours as she wanted. Also, Rhonda was always looking for someone to cover her shifts, which allowed Meshel to earn additional pay. Meshel was happy to be able to contribute to the bills and food at her brother Roland's apartment. While he didn't require this from her, he was happy to see his big sister taking her place in life, paying for her way and eventually for her own apartment. Each payday, Meshel ordered new clothing or toys online for Marcus and Ashton, her younger son. She would most of the times have the items delivered to Roland's apartment in Connecticut and other times to her job in Manhattan where she worked. Occasionally, whenever she had the weekend off, she would spend time with her sons at Roland's apartment in Connecticut.

Rhonda was still a bit of a roughneck, her games evolved for desperate people like Meshel, perfectly matched to be spun in the web like all her workers. Rhonda's system placed desperate women to work her shifts, for which these women were compelled to give her a portion of their pay back to her in return. Rhonda was a charmer and a conniver. She convinced her employers that she had legitimate emergencies to cover her absences. Meanwhile, her pay-for-work system worked flawlessly, sometimes for months at a time.

Rhonda barely had to lift a finger to work. She had more than enough women willing to work her shifts while she sat back, taking their payments to fund her chic lifestyle. Her brutish nature, however, caused her many reprisals that disallowed her the enjoyment of her luxuries in peace. She began to increase her fees-for-work, "Any lady that wants another lady's shift, must clear her exchange with me first. She advanced her demands on her workers. If you give up your shift to another lady, I have to be paid a fee for re-coordinating the schedules." Many of the ladies complained behind her back.

Meshel was passionate about her work. Taking care of the elderly reminded her of her grandmother Brownie, she was reminded of Brownie's great conversations, advice, wisdom, the only difference was that her clients also shared salacious tid-bits of their past sexual trysts! Meshel was quite surprised to learn that the elderly still had strong urges to do freaky things.

Thanksgiving weekend was approaching, and Meshel had been working for a solid month without a single day off, so she asked Rhonda for relief. She needed to spend the holidays with her boys.

"Meshel, a little holiday, and you want to leave the job already? You don't know how to make money, girl, so let me call this new lady. I'll call you back, okay?" Rhonda responded with her typical plucky attitude.

Rhonda sent Trisha to relieve Meshel. Just like Meshel, Trisha was eager to work, but she was only in her second month working through Rhonda. She had no children, but she had already lost patience with Rhonda's work arrangement. Meshel and Trisha chatted for a while, and Trisha was not as forgiving nor grateful as Meshel for Rhonda's help-for-pay work arrangement. Trisha was from Trinidad and Tobago and had no problem venting her frustration to her Bajan co-worker Meshel.

"Meshel, we Caribbean ladies shouldn't be like that with one another! Why is Rhonda expecting more money from you because I came to be your relief? She's taking advantage of us, and I strongly believe it might be illegal. In fact, a friend of mine called it extortion at its highest level." Trisha was fed up with Rhonda's greed, "I'm already at the point to tell her NO MORE MONEY! I have given you enough 'thank you's' from my paycheck."

Meshel was a bit worried that Trisha was about to spark a revolution against Rhonda. "Trisha, maybe you and Rhonda should talk in private to resolve the issue."

Trisha's flame was already lit for Rhonda, "Meshel, I'm calling her after Thanksgiving is over. What do you think?" Trisha ranted on-and-on, putting Meshel on the spot for an opinion.

Then it finally dawned on Meshel, You know what? Maybe Trisha might be the perfect person to put Rhonda in her place. "Trisha, I can't disagree with you. Go with God's grace."

"Thank you, Meshel. Go enjoy your holidays with your boys. I can tell they miss you. You've been gone a whole month; I don't know how you do it."

Monday night after Thanksgiving weekend, Meshel was back at her job with her client. Her cell phone rang, and it was Rhonda. "Hey, Rhonda?"

"Meshel, can you believe those ungrateful heffas!" Rhonda blurted out, not waiting for a response before continuing. "They don't want to pay my fees. What are they thinking? I should work for free?"

What you do is hardly considered work, Meshel thought to herself.

"I got them all jobs, and I got you a job. Why shouldn't I get paid for it?" Rhonda went on-and-on. "You don't complain, but now this new girl Trisha wants to start complaining. They should all be like you and be grateful for what I do for you all."

It was evident that Rhonda mistook Meshel's silence for agreement. Maintaining her composure Meshel asked, "Rhonda, do you really think you're being fair?"

"Of course I am!" Rhonda replied feeling offended.

For the first time Rhonda was exposed to Meshel's sharp logical mind, "I do agree that you should be paid a fee for finding us jobs. And I might not personally care about the fee you charge for switching shifts. But endless fees, Rhonda, are really unfair!" Meshel voiced her opinion, calmly and soft-toned.

Rhonda was silent for a moment, then she spoke, "So my loyal lioness has also turned on me like the rest of these Hyenas? I remember your sister and my sister were going to fight, now you want to start with me? Feisty Meshel was when they were younger. Rhonda mistook Meshel's silence for weakness, she realized it in that one moment. Still, she wasn't willing to admit any wrong and she wasn't ready to back down either.

Meshel continued to apply pressure, she asked again, "Seriously, Rhonda, do you think you're being fair? Perhaps they should only pay you for the first two weeks, but that leads me to another question. When you started doing this work many years ago, you said the lady who helped you also charged you a fee. Are you still paying her a fee?" Rhonda's response was silence! Meshel asked again, "Seriously, Rhonda, are you still paying a fee to the lady that helped you get your first job many years ago?"

Rhonda evaded the question, continued her rant, "This is not fair to me! I can't believe this is happening again! I have to tell Aunt Rose about this. All of you are so ungrateful! You all just want to take from me and give nothing back. You all have no conscience! God, don't like ugly, you hear me? God don't like ugly! And you Meshel, you are the worst out of all these women! You've been quiet all this time, and now you're against me?"

That late Tuesday morning, Meshel began getting phone calls from Rhonda's Aunt Rose. Meshel was one of the few ladies Rhonda hired, that Aunt Rose called. Aunt Rose, the gangstress, threatened Meshel, "Pay Rhonda her money! Don't be ungrateful! Don't let me have to come up to your job and see you about this!"

"Pay her what, Rose? I've been more than fair to your niece. I think we all have been. Oh, and by the way, if you show up here at my job, I will call the police on you!" Meshel slapped back.

"Snitch!" shrieked Aunt Rose

Meshel saw right through her bluff. Rose had a slew of legal troubles looming over her head, so she didn't want another encounter with the police. She sucked her teeth in anger, then ended the call abruptly with Meshel.

Meshel continued to work through Rhonda. The tension was thick, but both women avoided confrontation. Rhonda continued her unfair practices, and Meshel paid what she had to. She was focused on a more important goal and would not allow Rhonda's drama to get in her way. Just like they did in high school, they avoided fighting, but they weren't friends.

CHAPTER 41

TWENTY SOMETHING

Lemar met Lisa at a company party thrown by friends who worked for a top national delivery service company. As soon as he saw her his immediate thought was, she is gorgeous! Lisa's chocolate brown skin complimented her hour-glass figure. The way she swirled her body made Lemar think she had to be good at dancing. Lemar studied her movements and her presence for a while, then he decided, I need to dance with her. Her hips moved in tune to his 2-step rhythm, she had experience. Then the DJ played a slower song, surprisingly Lisa pressed her body against Lemar's muscular frame. Their bodies flowed as they rocked back and forth. Lisa's Chloe perfume spiked Lemar's senses. The ease with which Lemar navigated her movements elevated her interest. Lemar asked, "Would you like something to drink?"

"Yes. Water, please." Lisa responded, smiling to show perfectly whitened teeth.

They headed to the makeshift bar, and Lemar asked for two bottles of sparkling alkaline spring water. He guided Lisa to an open bar-height table, opened her bottle, and handed it to her. "I'm Lemar." He stuck out his hand.

"Lisa." She shook his hand.

Wow! What a firm handshake. Lemar thought.

"I haven't seen you around before. Are you new?" Lisa asked.

"I've been with the company for about a year. But this is my first company party." Lemar replied.

"Oh. Okay. So, you're a full-time employee with benefits and a retirement plan. Okay, I see you." Lisa joked.

Lemar raised an eyebrow but laughed along with her joke.

They chatted for a while and shared stories about their past. Lemar learned that she was five years his senior and had been with her company for nine years. Lisa also lived with her father because her mother had recently passed away, and she was worried about how her older, though not elderly, father would survive by himself. Lemar was simply thrilled to find out she was single and interested in dating. They exchanged phone numbers before Lisa left the party.

Lemar and Lisa were inseparable for a while. He spent a great deal of time visiting her at her father's house. He developed a friendly relationship with her father and helped them with some of the maintenance needed around the house. Lemar wanted to elevate their relationship further, so he tested the waters by asking Lisa if she would be willing to buy a home with him in the future. He was, however, met with resistance, "I can't leave my dad, he'll be all alone.

"My dad needs me, Lemar," Lisa proclaimed further.

"He'll be okay, Lisa. At some point, you have to get your own place. We can't keep sleeping in your childhood bedroom," Lemar urged.

"I know, but now is not the right time for me to leave him."

Lisa pleaded, hoping Lemar would understand.

"You seem like you're more interested in staying here to punish your father for cheating on your mother. You're not helping him!" Lemar pointed out.

"That's not true, Lemar. I am trying to help my dad. Besides, I told you, when I lived with my ex-boyfriend, he lied and cheated on me, and I don't want to go through that again." Lisa said, defending her stance.

"I'm not your ex, and I'm not your father! You have to get over your trust issues, Lisa!" Lemar argued.

Lemar understood that Lisa carried some emotional scars from her past relationship. Her ex-boyfriend was her first real love, and they were engaged to be married. He cheated on her throughout their entire relationship. Lisa witnessed how physically sick life with a cheating husband could make a woman. She witnessed her mother's declining health from putting up with years of her father's infidelity. Her mother made Lisa swear never to put herself in the same situation. Once her mother passed away, Lisa was certain to live up to her promise and decided to break off her engagement. While Lemar was empathetic to Lisa's past, he was tired of putting his life on hold. Six years passed, and Lisa was still unwilling to leave her father. Lemar grew weary of trying to convince her to leave and decided it was time to move on.

Lemar rebounded quickly when he met Kim, a registered

nurse who had recently moved to New York City from her southern home in Lovejoy, Georgia. Kim was warm and laid back. She'd grown up with both of her parents, who adorned her with love. Kim's parents were the opposite of Lisa's parents, leaving Kim void of no obvious baggage from childhood trauma.

Kim and Lemar soon got engaged and were married two years after they met. Matthew Jones officiated the ceremony, witnessed and attended by almost two-hundred family members and friends. A year later, Kim gave birth to their twin girls, Mia and Nia, who were his little inspirations, his little star lights. Each night after their birth, while they were asleep, Lemar consistently leaned over his daughters and whispered the Lord's prayer.

Lemar was determined to do all he could for his family. Home life was loving and warm, and things flowed well until the twins were about three years old. Kim's attitude started to change until it became completely unrecognizable. She became cold and distant. She worked longer hours than usual, and when she came home, she retreated into their bedroom or an unoccupied room to be alone. She didn't engage much with her daughters and was hardly interested in having sex with Lemar. Initially, Lemar wondered if she was suffering from postpartum depression. He convinced Kim to see a Therapist to determine the cause of her aberrant mood swings. The therapist, however, declared that Kim was angry with her parents and jealous of her daughters.

Lemar didn't understand Kim's anger with her parents. He thought deeply about their relationship; from his vantage point, they had a great connection. He gave Kim the best of everything to support her dreams. He was also perplexed as to why she was jealous of her own daughters. Lemar sought to understand what his wife was going through, but each time he tried to talk about it, she became extremely defensive, and it only turned into an argument. He tried to get Kim to see that her behavior was affecting their daughters, hoping that her motherly instincts to protect her children would kick in.

On a rare weekday afternoon when Kim was home, she dressed her younger Nia for the park while Lamar dressed Mia as the elder. Nia kept looking back and forth between Kim and her father. Then she settled her stare into her mother's eyes and asked, "Mommy, what are you doing here for?" Kim was astonished, and so was Lamar, then Lemar realized it was Nia's reaction to Kim's constant absences; most times, it was Lemar who dressed Nia and her sister. *This has gone too far. I've got to do something.* Lemar thought, pondering his plan for an intervention.

Upcoming summer and Kim's parents were scheduled to visit with them from Georgia. Lemar was both excited and edgy about their visit. Mia and Nia loved their grandparents who spoiled them rotten, that usually made Kim very upset with her parents. At the beginning of their summer visit, Kim's connection with her parents seemed normal, but with each family activity and social event, Kim began building up a wall against their presence. She showed less interest in being a part of any family activities or socializing.

"Why is Kim acting this way?" her mother asked Lemar.

"I'm not sure, but I hoped you and dad could keep the girls this weekend so I could take Kim for a quick weekend getaway." Lemar answered.

Kim's parents were excited to have the girls for the weekend. Mia and Nia looked forward to their grandparents spoiling them all weekend.

Lemar and Kim packed their bags, heading off for some much-needed time alone at a bed-and-breakfast near some wineries in upstate New York. The scenery of the Hudson River Valley through the huge, bay windows was breathtaking, the room was tranquil with a cool travertine tiled balcony. It was the perfect backdrop for a romantic and peaceful weekend. At first, Kim seemed relaxed and welcomed the time alone with Lemar.

"Thank you for coming up here with me, my love," Lemar said.

"Thank you, sweetheart. I needed this," she responded.

"It's been a while since we had this perfect vibe to make love. It's been way too long." Lemar confessed.

"And I'm ready for you!" Kim exclaimed.

His wife's response totally aroused Lemar. It's on now! he

thought to himself as he cozied up with Kim. Their flaming passions made the silk sheets too hot as Lemar repeatedly rocked her little man in the boat deep into the night. They released their energies until they slept, awakened in the morning by the sounds of the summer birds chirping and tweeting their melodies. They tried to outdo each other with intensity and ecstasy, just like old times. Kim's fire and passion for Lemar were clearly still here, but her passion for her family was waning, flickering like a lit candle bothered by an ongoing breeze from an unknown source.

"Knock-knock!" It was room service at the door.

"Oh-ooh. Were we too loud?" Kim whispered laughingly to Lemar. As Lemar opened the door he was unexpectedly greeted with the aroma of turkey bacon, eggs, Belgian waffles, fresh fruit, and fresh brewed coffee tantalizing their senses of smell. They took turns feeding each other fresh fruit and kissed the drizzled nectar from each other's lips and chins, down to their chests and even lower. After breakfast, Lemar thought there wasn't a better time than now to ask Kim about her disconnect with their daughters. *She's in a good mood. We are relaxing and don't have to rush anywhere. Now should be a good time.* Lemar pondered, convincing himself to make his move.

"Luv, I'm so happy to see you laughing again. I've been missing your smile," Lemar admitted.

"It does feel good to laugh," Kim admitted.

"I'd like to see you smile and laugh more at home. I'm sure

the girls would like that too." Lemar proposed cunningly.

"I do laugh and smile at home! What do you mean, smile more?" Kim snapped.

Lemar felt her anger rising. Her joyfulness became flustered. Her smile faded as her lips pursed to express her irritation.

"I'm not saying that you don't laugh and smile at all, Luv. I'm just saying it would be good if the girls could see you do it more often." Lemar said again, trying to soften the impact and tone of his words.

"Well, I don't feel like laughing and smiling with them all the time." Kim admitted.

Paradise was now lost, Kim's response pulled at Lemar's heartstrings. She inflamed his emotions, and he raised his voice at her, "What does that mean?" He snapped back at her.

"It means I don't feel like being bothered!" Kim snapped again.

"Why not? We are blessed with two beautiful girls who love us. Why wouldn't you 'feel like being bothered?'" Lemar said mockingly as he quoted her words back to her.

Kim fell silent. She sighed and stared blankly at Lemar. He sensed that she was holding something back and wondered what it had to do with their daughters.

"What's wrong, Luv? Talk to me." He urged, with a much calmer tone, desperate to know the truth.

Kim took in a deep breath as tears swelled in her eyes, "I've been mad at my parents for years, Lemar!" she said, tears streamed down her soft cheeks as she started to cry silently.

"Why? Mad at them for what? What did they do? What does this have to do with our girls?" Lemar was confused and wanted answers. Meanwhile, he took tissues and dabbed her tears.

"I never had a childhood! They made me study all the time! Spelling Bees, debate club, biology club, psychology club, this club, that club, it was TOO MUUUCH!" Now she cried out loud. "Sometimes it made me feel like I wanted to club them."

"Okayyy." Lemar was still confused but kept his silence, leaving the air open for her to continue. He remembered his Spelling Bee experience, chaperone, Miss Jones, and proctor, Mr. Andrews. It wasn't that bad, he thought.

"I couldn't have a boyfriend; my dad chased them all away. As soon as I had the opportunity to leave, I did. I had to get away and just wanted to be free."

Lemar was still confused but didn't want to seem insensitive to her feelings. However, he was more concerned about what any of this had to do with their daughters. His frustration grew as he waited for Kim to shed light on his real concern. He stood quietly and listened intently.

"I thought I was free when I moved to New York City, but they continued to hound me. 'When are you getting married?'

'When are you going to give us some grandchildren?' The interrogation never ended, and it was exhausting." Kim expressed with exasperation.

"But what does this have to do with our girls?" Lemar pressed on, refusing to give up.

"I'm jealous of them, okay?" Kim blurted. "I didn't get the chance to be like them, dance classes, tea parties, swimming lessons, fun with mommy and daddy. I didn't have a real childhood. Now I have to be a real mother, wife, and nurse to people, when all I wish I could do is be someone's little girl again, and I want to be treated the way you treat our daughters.

"Are you angry at your parents for making you successful?" Lemar asked. Oh damn, that sounded insensitive, he thought.

"Yeah, they made me successful all right, but they ruined my life! They ruined my childhood!" Kim now cried aloud.

This time Lemar took two steps back mentally, he chose his words with more empathy. He never knew this much about Kim's perception of her childhood; he certainly didn't realize that seeing their daughters' happiness would trigger so much pain in her being. "Kim, it's going to be okay. We can get through this together. Just trust me, as I've always trusted you. Our girls need you, and they need us."

Lemar embraced his wife, but something was missing. Her hug felt empty. Was she so far gone? He feared nothing would be the same again between them.

Two years later, Kim filed for divorce, dragging Lemar into an ugly court battle. Kim's parents were at her side and helped her fight for sole custody of her girls. Lemar was furious because, for the past three years, he supplemented the love Kim refused to give them due to her issues with her parents. Now she wants to take my girls from me! He refused to allow Kim to take them back to Georgia to live with her parents. So, they settled on living in two separate houses and shared joint custody.

Lemar had his girls every other weekend. On his off weekends, his schedule was full of plans preparing for the weekends they'd be with him. After he completed decorating and furnishing their rooms, he built a swing set and a slide. Their grandmother got them into painting their nails with glitter, so when he brought them a nail polish kit, he became their mannequin for nail polishing practice and other girl-dad activities.

Kim's relationship with her daughters improved, but it took a few years of Lemar managing or ignoring her angry outbursts and at times callous decisions. Finally Kim realized within herself, I need to stop hurting myself and my babies! Still, she struggled, as she still yearned for the love that a child receives when they're young. She struggled to find true love with a new beau, her unresolved issues of self-love kept her in short -lived entanglements, fleeting overrated love trysts. She found it increasingly difficult to find what she thought she was looking for, a surrogate daddy in place of a real hubby.

BACK TO THE

BOOKSTORE

One sunny afternoon in upper Manhattan while on a call from work, Lemar's eyes came upon a uniquely beautiful woman. She had wild yet tamed curly jet-black hair. Her body was curvy, and the slightest hew of makeup delicately complimented her facial features. She carried herself gracefully but had a serious demeanor. Lemar couldn't help but stare at this brown butterfly as she walked in his direction. He was so smitten by her beauty that he almost didn't notice anyone else, then he bumped into another man on the sidewalk.

"Watch out, buddy!" the man called out.

"Oh, I'm sorry, sir!" Lemar turned to apologize to the man. He quickly spun back around to admire this alluring woman; but just like that, poof! She was gone. Where did she go? Lemar spun around in a complete circle, but she was nowhere to be found.

As Lemar worked through the day, he kept his eyes open for this gem of a woman he saw earlier. To his dismay, she never re-appeared. Later that day, his boss called again and asked if he could do a quick job at a nearby bookstore since he was already in the area. Lemar agreed, packed his tools into his work truck, and headed towards the bookstore.

Lemar was an avid reader, so working on an assignment in a bookstore was a welcomed opportunity. He had a pretty healthy library of books at home but was always game to add more books to his collection. After completing his job, Lemar decided to stroll around the bookstore a bit, see what new titles he might purchase. His reading interests varied; he had a few genres he loved for various reasons. As he strolled through the aisles, he spotted another woman standing in the Health and Beauty aisle with a coffee cup in one hand, and a magazine in the other. Lemar stopped dead in his tracks. Wait a minute? Could that be my brown butterfly that I saw earlier? It looks like her. Let me get closer to her so I can see better.

CHAPTER 43

CROSSING PATHS

The bookstore's in-house coffee shop was one of Meshel's favorite places to read. There was something about the aroma of freshly brewed coffee and the smell of fresh paper swathed in the books on the shelves. Meshel frequently visited this local bookstore in her neighborhood. Her first stop was always the café bar before heading to the health and beauty section to grab the latest fashion magazines, health journals, or biographical novels for her next reading selection.

This sunny afternoon, Meshel continued her familiar bookstore routine. As she stood in the aisle reading up on the latest fashion trends, she noticed a very handsome man standing at the end of the bookshelves. So she lifted her head, just so she could see that he was smiling at her. Wow! He is handsome, she found herself thinking. At first, she turned to see who was behind her; perhaps he was smiling at someone else? But then she realized she was the only person in the aisle, and apparently, he was smiling at her. So she smiled back. As Lemar stepped into the aisle, Meshel noticed his heavily worn work clothes, *what kind of dirty work does he do?* She thought as she frowned a bit. Lemar caught her look of disapproval, he felt a tad self-conscious and glanced down at his work clothes, but he wasn't giving up on meeting 'brown butterfly.' *Oh boy. I hope she's not thinking I'm some kind of bum.*

"Hello," Meshel said as Lemar walked toward her. She wanted to take control of the conversation before he spoke, just to see how exactly brave he was.

"Hello," Lemar responded quite simply, unbothered by her assertive disposition.

Meshel then waited for him to say something else. She stood silent, as Lemar also stood silent in an awkward moment, but he didn't stop staring at her in admiration. Lemar was actually speechless for the next few moments, so Meshel asked, "Are you looking for someone?"

"I certainly am. I saw you on the street earlier today, and I was surprised just now to see you in the store." Said Lemar, still smiling from ear-to-ear.

Meshel took notice of Lemar's physique, his muscular build. She also noticed that his hair was neatly cut, and his fingernails were clean. Hmmm, good, she thought.

"Okay. Is there something I can help you with? And in case you're wondering, I don't work here," Meshel said. She kept him frozen in his tracks, almost as if she were shining a bright flashlight in his eyes.

"I was just wondering what kind of books you like to read?" Lemar asked.

"Ummm, and how is that any of your business?" Meshel asked. She held back her smile as she realized how shy Lemar was as he attempted to flirt with her.

"Because I think it's important to know something about a

woman's mind and not just her pretty appearance," Lemar said, charmingly as he began to regain his mental footing under her little interrogation.

"Are you trying to say that I'm pretty?" Meshel teased.

Lemar answered, matter of factly. "Yes. I think you're beautiful."

"Well, why didn't you just say that from the beginning." Meshel sassed, no longer able to hide her big bright smile.

He stretched out his arm to shake Meshel's hand, "I'm Lemar."

"Meshel," she returned his gesture. *Hmm, strong hands.* She thought.

Lemar and Meshel stood in the aisle. Almost nothing else in the world mattered for the next thirty minutes as they talked until Lemar's cell phone rang again.

"I'm sorry, Meshel, excuse me for a second, duty calls," he answered his phone… "Oh boy, I have to get over to another job site," he informed her.

"No worries. I understand. Work pays the bills, right?" Meshel chuckled.

Lemar put his phone number in Meshel's phone, and left her while pleading with her, "please call me?"

"I will." Meshel replied.

"I'm holding you to that," said Lemar, as he slowly retreated from her, turning around just at the end of the aisle to walk away and leave the bookstore.

In two separate places, yet underneath the same moonlit night that evening, Meshel and Lemar replayed their time together in their thoughts.

CHAPTER 44

VACATION

Lemar and Meshel dated over the next few weeks. They spent all their free time together and talked on the phone for hours whenever they couldn't see each other. Meshel's schedule was hectic, between work and visiting her sons on her weekends off. Lemar was just as tied up between work and his girls, however, he wanted to spend some uninterrupted time with Meshel.

"I want to take you on a little vacation. Can you take about five days off from work?" Lemar was hoping she would say yes.

Meshel was excited about going on a vacation with Lemar. She coordinated coverage for her shifts at work and set out to spend the next five days with her new love beau. As they set out for the anticipated thirteen-hour drive down the East Coast, Lemar turned on his favorite R&B XM station. Not more than an hour into the ride, Meshel's cell phone began to ring, her fill-in person calling from her job. Looking at the caller ID, she thought, *at least I'm not like Rhonda, "Don't call me" because she didn't care*. Lemar understood the importance but was still annoyed as this was supposed to be their dedicated time together. Meshel remained on the call for almost two hours, then complained about her battery dying, realizing she forgot to pack her charger.

Aha, this was Lemar's chance to keep her attention focused on him. "Sorry, I don't have a car charger for your type of cell phone." Meshel suspected Lemar might be lying but went along with it anyway. She appreciated his determination to keep them focused on their time together and avoid any distractions. She rested her head on the seat, let the wind blow through her curly tresses, and hummed along to the sultry tunes of the music.

Lemar glimpsed Meshel looking at her phone from time to time. He knew it would be difficult to get her mind off work. Being at work became her life. She explained to him how much she depended on her job to care for her boys and build up enough money to get her own place so she could be with them more. Lemar didn't want to interrupt her talk, but he wanted to help ease her stress because he believed everyone needs a break from work. He admired her hustle and determination, but he was more intrigued by her innocence; she was the kind of woman that piqued his curiosity. Lemar's heart was growing fond of Meshel, so he made plans to keep her in his life, keeping her happy and secure along the way.

Time to diminish her distractions, he thought. "So tell me more about your mother. You said she died years ago, but what was she like? What can I see in you that came from her?"

Meshel was pleasantly shocked. She paused for a moment and thought none of these other men ever asked me such a question. He actually wants to know about my mother. "Well, she worked hard to take care of me, my brothers, and my sisters."

Lemar politely interrupted, "I can see that in you already. I guess you got your work ethic from your mom?"

Meshel smiled and acknowledged, "I guess I did." Then she

continued, "My mother did make some terrible mistakes, though, when it came to men. After my father, she put the next man she was with before us." Meshel sighed, "I hated that man Mr. Milton!"

Lemar asked, "So, how do you and your siblings get along? How do you...."

"Siblings?" Meshel interrupted and teased Lemar, "You speak so proper sometimes. You mean my brothers and sisters? Yeah, we all get along great. Sometimes they get on my nerves, and I do the same, but we still love each other."

Lemar didn't particularly like being mocked about his English, and he wasn't modest about his use of unusual words during conversations, but he laughed it off and said, "Well, I guess You'll have to get used to my proper English. But it is good to hear that you and your 'brothers and sisters,'" [imitating her], "...get along."

"So, do you have any siblings? Do y'all...I meant to say... Do you all get along?" Meshel and Lemar laughed, realizing they shared a kindred sense of humor.

"Yes. I have twin brothers named Ainsley and Anton. They're from my mother's second marriage, and they're fifteen years younger than I am; but we have a great relationship." Lemar shared.

"Oh wow, that's cool that you have a good relationship with

your brothers."

Lemar paused and gave some thought before sharing further. "I recently found out that I have an older sister."

"Really?" Meshel asked. She was shocked at the revelation because she was under the impression that Lemar's family wouldn't be the type to have such drama. Then she remembered his parents did get divorced so there had to be some reasons behind it.

"Yeah. My father told me he had a girlfriend before he met my mother. His girlfriend got pregnant, but her parents didn't think my father was good enough for her to marry, so they sent her to England to give birth and live with family members. So, my sister has lived her entire life in England, and my dad didn't get to see her until she was a teenager. I was about ten years old when she came to stay with us for a month. We had a great time getting to know each other. But yeah…that's the story of my siblings."

They looked at each other and burst out laughing as they said, "siblings," both at the same time.

"Well, we don't have any control over the siblings we have. My mother had my little sisters by old nasty Mr. Milton, but we love them regardless of their father. They're twins. I'm also very close to my younger sister, Pamela, and my younger brother, Roland. Many people say I got my temper from my mother and my looks from my father." Meshel gloated.

Temper? Oh boy, I don't want to deal with a hot-tempered person. Lemar was concerned, his eyebrows raised, and his temples quivered.

"Temper, huh? Sooo then you're a hothead?" he immediately asked.

Feeling a little embarrassed, Meshel quickly explained. "Well, I wouldn't say a hothead. I've always been the most outspoken among my brothers and sisters, and it always got me in trouble with my mother." Meshel paused... "I had to speak up! She made some really bad decisions that affected all of us, and somebody needed to hold her accountable."

"Accountable? Now look who's using their vocabulary." Lemar teased. He looked over and noticed her eyes were heavy with tears.

Meshel's voice quivered a little, as she confessed, "I regret the time I told my mother I hated her. I wish I never said it."

"I'm sure she knew you didn't mean it," Lemar reassured her, offering comfort as he reached over and wiped the tears from her cheeks with his bare fingers. She grabbed his hand, still moist with tears, held it for a second, pressed his hand against her cheek, then kissed his hand. That moment marked the beginning of a deeper connection between them both.

They talked more about their past lives, children, goals, and dreams. They shared their religious beliefs and enjoyed learning how much they had in common. Meshel occasionally stared out the window and absorbed the serene scenery. Lemar couldn't help but think, could she really be the one?

CHAPTER 45

NELLIE

Meshel and Lemar's relationship blossomed, and it became the envy of their friends and their relatives as their love stood the test of time. They experienced love like they never had in past relationships. Aside from the occasional petty quarrels, they hadn't faced any real difficulty in their commitment to one another. So, like any other relationship, the test of fidelity was on the verge of emerging.

Meshel shared some of her work responsibilities and shifts with her colleague, Nellie. However, over time their association blossomed into a close friendship. Of course, confident and intimate details about their private lives were also shared between them. Nellie was married, but often shared with Meshel stories of her secret entanglements with other men. Meshel found Nellie's stories somewhat sleazy, but entertaining, notwithstanding she still disagreed with Nellie's cheating. *Who am I to tell a grown woman what to do with her body?* Meshel thought to herself. However, Meshel took a soft heart toward Nellie's situation because she was aware of the physical abuse Nellie endured at the hands of her husband. Nellie's outlet was to seek solace and revenge while in the arms of other men in bed, in cars, and even in public.

Nellie loved hearing Meshel's fascinating tales of her romance and escapades with Lemar. She often asked Meshel to re-tell details of her stories like they were episodes of her own fantasies, over and over again. Her pretense of genuine happiness for Meshel would be short lived, because Meshel's stories inflamed her curiosity, leading into jealousy. She was a snake willing to shed her skin or her clothing, carrying venom with her slippery tongue before she bit her victims with her seductions. One day while she overheard Lemar and Meshel chatting over the phone during Meshel's lunch break at work, Nellie sought to identify any weakness she could exploit to ruin their relationship.

"Sometimes I feel like this relationship is too good to be true," Meshel confessed to Nellie.

"Girl, you know how many women would love to be in your shoes?" Nellie agreed with Meshel, just to encourage her to say more.

"I'm sure, Lemar is a good man," Meshel said as she thought about his qualities.

"Do you feel like you don't deserve him though?" Nellie probed further.

Meshel pondered for a minute, "Sometimes I do. I wonder what he really thinks about my past drama?" She admits to Nellie.

"I think he sees you beyond all of your past drama. Why would you doubt that?" Nellie asked, hoping for a solid opening she could use to gain Lemar's attention.

"I'm not sure. He's just not like anyone I've dated," Meshel answered.
"Do you think he would cheat on you?" Nellie cunningly asked.

"Of course not! Not really. Well…I hope not. Hmmm…I don't know," Meshel went from confident to unsure in a matter of seconds. This was the blemish in the fabric Nellie had been hoping to find.

"Girl, let me tell you that man is not going to cheat on you," Nellie said disingenuously. "Uhm, sorry to change the subject, but I forgot that I don't have a ride to the bus station come Friday night, so I may not be able to work the day shift. You're probably going to have to come in to cover me Friday morning," Nellie knew Meshel usually spent time with Lemar before coming in for her shift and would not be happy if she had to work during their quality time.

"Oh no, Nellie! You know that's my time with Lem," Meshel frowned.

"I know Meshel, but I don't have a ride, so there's nothing I can do. Unless. . .you know what, never mind," Nellie sulked.

"Unless, what?" Meshel was all ears to hear Nellie's suggestion.

"It might be asking too much, but I'm just trying to think of a way to not interfere with you and Lemar's time together," said Nellie conspiring quite coyly.

"Nellie, stop! What are you thinking?" Meshel was frustrated, wishing Nellie would just say out loud what was on her mind.

"Well, if Lemar can drive me to the bus station after my shift when he drops you off, then I can come in and not interfere with your time," Nellie persuasively suggested.

"You know what, let me ask him and get back to you. I'm sure he won't have a problem with it." Meshel responded.

"Riiight. 'Cause he is a 'gentleman,'" Nellie said mockingly as they both burst into laughter.

Lemar agreed to drive Nellie to the bus station after dropping Meshel to work, "No problem, Luv. It's on my way to the highway anyway."

Meshel was thrilled to tell Nellie. Therefore, she would have no interruptions of her time with Lemar. Nellie was just as excited. Finally, I can get him alone. Ms. Goodie-Goodie thinks her man is so perfect. Well, we're about to see how true it is. Nellie exhaled as she fantasized about seducing Lemar.

Friday evening came, Lemar dropped Meshel off at work and waited in his vehicle for Nellie. Meshel returned with Nellie and introduced them.

"Lemar, this is my friend, Nellie. Nellie, this is my baby, Lemar," Meshel gloated.

"Hi, Nellie. I've heard a lot about you. Nice to meet you," Lemar said, being polite, as he thought of her salacious ways.

"Likewise, she's always talking about you, and I just had to meet you for myself," Nellie said with a sly smirk.

Meshel was usually skeptical of some people's intentions, but she wasn't quite tuned in to the subtle signs of Nellie's intended deceit. While she didn't trust Nellie totally, she knew Lemar was different. Lemar was nonchalant about Nellie because he had seen pictures of her and didn't find her that attractive in photos, so he went along with Meshel's request to drive her friend to the bus station. He'd heard stories of Nellie's debauchery and secret escapades. He wasn't too fond of Meshel hanging around with a promiscuous married woman, but he believed Meshel had integrity. He kissed Meshel goodnight, and as they lovingly parted, a little French kissing occurred. Nellie blushed while hopping into the front passenger seat. She waved a quick goodbye to Meshel, and now she was ready to act on her intentions with Lemar.

Nellie was unusually dressed, instead of her usual casual baggy jeans and sweatshirt, she wore instead a blue wild-rose Bohemian midi dress that looked somewhat casual but provided easy access for her other plans. She also wore a thong and easy access push-up bra underneath, just to set the mood for herself before her featured drive to the bus station with Lemar. Nellie often came across as timid, the type some women would think they could trust around their men, that was her game. She even pretended at times to be dimwitted as she knew it would make people think her to be no threat to anyone. She sat in the passenger seat, crouching like a lioness, waiting for the right moment to pounce at Lemar for his sexual attention. Lemar's eyes instead, were fixed on the road ahead, as he drove off to Nellie's bus station.

He's being too quiet, Nellie thought. I need him to speak to me. So she asked, "Do you have any of your music in the car?"

Feeling a bit surprised that she already knew about his music, Lemar said cordially, "Yeah. I have some, plus some mixes I created myself. Meshel must have told you how much I love music."

"Yes. She tells me everything about you," Nellie said provocatively. For the first time, Lemar looked over at her as she spoke, so Nellie took the opportunity to look him directly in his eyes while playing with her hair, just to give him the message that she was open for an even deeper interaction. "How much time do you have?" She asked.

Lemar was slightly confused by the question, so he responded curiously, "Why do you ask?"

"I just wondered what it is you do with all that time after you drop off Meshel?" said Nellie seductively.

"Well, I usually talk to her on the phone while I drive, and we stay on the phone until duty calls for her at work." Lemar shared. "So, after I drop you off, I'll call her, and We'll talk for as long as we can."

What could they have to talk about like that? They just finished spending time together. Nellie wondered, feeling slightly flushed; her temple pulsed, and her heartbeat palpitated from jealousy. She remembered when her husband used to adore her the same way. She held back her sadness and tears, then pressed forward with her deceitful plot. Nellie coped with her heartache by learning to prey on other men. She found it to be a magical distraction. Most of the men she coerced and seduced were either unhappily married or a bit insecure with themselves, just happy to be chosen by such a seductive and passionate woman. She'd mastered the art of seduction, easily detecting these weakened men. However, Lemar was going to be different. He wasn't married, nor was he insecure. He was quite handsome to some women and cute to others, besides which, he was used to being around a beautiful sexy woman, like Meshel. After all, Meshel was stunning and had a great body; most of all, she adored him. Nellie already knew that she was up for a challenge, as she wasn't Meshel's equal in the beauty or the body arena.

"Well, my bus isn't for another hour and forty-five minutes. I'm starving! Do you think we could stop for something to eat?" Nellie asked, sounding as innocent as she could.

"Oh, I don't think so. Meshel is going to flip if she doesn't hear from me soon," Lemar replied. Why would I call Meshel while I'm out eating with her friend? Lemar thought.

"Yeah, but I'm really hungry!" Nellie whined. She felt his rejection, tranquilizing her demons, but it didn't totally humble her soul.

Lemar's memory was jolted, then he pointed to a bag in the backseat of his vehicle. "Oh, yeah! Look in that bag on the back seat. Meshel told me she was ordering an extra beef shish kebab for you when we had lunch earlier."

Nellie rolled her eyes. Damn it! Why does Meshel have to think of everything? As she unbuckled her seatbelt, she stretched her body and legs across the seat, revealing what she thought would be sexiness for Lemar as she grabbed the bag. Lemar also whiffed her Chloe perfume, one of his favorites. Easing herself back into her seat, she ensured that her curves under her dress, including her jiggling butt cheeks, were seen with every maneuver. Lemar picked up on her body language and immediately felt annoyed. I know this woman is not trying to come on to me! Not that Lemar wouldn't recognize a great beauty in front of him, but for him, it wasn't even that type of party.

"You need to get home to your husband, right?"

"Gosh, Lemar! Meshel told me you were a gentleman, but I didn't know you were such a lame!" Nellie blurted out.

"Nellie. I'm pleased with the one I'm with." Lemar responded, trying not to hurt her feelings any further, but more worried about the consequences of this sexual tension Nellie brought into his space, especially with the 'ME TOO' movement on the rise in the media.

"Well, you all don't SEEM to try anything new. Perhaps you should try something new with me?" Nellie probed, hoping for some truth, hoping for that same opening in the fabric that she, or he, could rip through for her opportunity. She began to sink back into her seat, anticipating though not hoping to be rejected.

Lemar didn't respond; instead, he thought *if there's anything else new for me to try, it certainly wouldn't be with you.* He pressed the gas a little harder, pushing slightly the pace of his vehicle. He wanted Nellie out as soon as possible! I know Meshel didn't put this woman up to test me. Lemar fumed to himself. He couldn't wait to get Meshel on the phone.

As soon as they arrived at the bus station, Nellie gathered her belongings and her pride. Climbing out of Lemar's vehicle, she closed the passenger door behind her, saying, "goodbye!" without even turning her head to see Lemar's response. He exhaled as he drove off, relieved by the departing end of Nellie's advances. He was glad she was out of his vehicle. He called Meshel using a hands-free system and waited for her to answer.

Hi, you've reached Meshel. I can't come to the phone right now, so please leave a message, and I will call you back. He hung up and continued driving. About ten minutes later, his phone rang. Meshel's name glared across the dashboard. As he always did, he smiled when he saw her name, although he was still fuming over what took place with Nellie.

"Hello," Lemar answered shortly.

"Hi, babe," Meshel said, sensing by his tone something was wrong. She asked, "Are you okay?"

"Yeah. I'm fine. Well, not really. Do you know what your friend did?" Lemar was interrupted by the sound of Meshel's laughter. "What's so funny?" He asked.

"Lem, I just got off the phone with Nellie. She told me you shut her down. She said you were 'so laaame!'" Meshel laughed into the phone.

"Lame? Is that all she told you?" Lemar asked.

"No. She told me she tried to flirt with you, and you turned her down," Meshel confirmed.

"Oh, so you put her up to that, right?" Lemar's frustration surfaced.

"Of course not! I would never do something like that, Lemar," Meshel's tone became more solemn.

"I hope so. Because you know I'm not a whoremonger, right? I try not to get down like that," Lemar assured her, at the same time musing about his past.

"I have no doubt, babe," Meshel acknowledged. Wow, he really is serious about our relationship, she thought to herself and smiled.

CHAPTER 46

MEETING FAMILY

As Meshel and Lemar's relationship quickly blossomed, some family members and friends began throwing shade because of their jealousy. The newest relationship became the subject of their anger, for no apparent reason! Was it jealousy, feelings of betrayal, loss of access and control over their own personal agendas? Who knew the reason(s)? Meshel and Lemar continued to spend most of their spare time between work together, seldom able to share time with family or friends. Pamela and Estelle were frustrated with their sister because she constantly cut them off, if Lemar called on the other line, while they were actively chit-chatting on the phone. Lemar's mother, Viola, badgered him about his lack of time for her and her family. She realized against her strongest wishes that Lemar had found new love, and it hurt her to accept that she would have to take second-row seating, as his new relationship evolved.

Things intensified once their children, Mia, Nia, Marcus, and Ashton, became acquainted as they began spending as much time together as Meshel and Lemar could muster. Charleston asked Marcus about the new man in Meshel's life, it seemed he was not quite over their past relationship. Meanwhile, Kim moaned about the twins being so acquainted with Meshel. Nevertheless, none of that really mattered to Meshel or Lemar; they were blissfully happy and wanted their children to be a part of their intended long-term relationship.

Meshel met the elder of Lamar's twin brothers Ainsley. Ainsley was not very good at expressing his emotions regarding family issues. His replies were often concise, and when pushed for more input, he deflected to his favorite scapegoat topics of sports or politics. He didn't engage very well on emotional levels, at least not with Lemar and his parents, but he was a happily married man. Meshel's encounter with Ainsley was very lackluster.

"Hey, Meshel. Nice to meet you. I've got to run. My wife's expecting me back home soon." Ainsley sputtered to her, hastening to depart without further conversation.

Meshel was flabbergasted. "He's leaving already? Lemar, is your brother okay? That was very rude!" She demanded a response from Lemar, glaring her eyes directly into his eyes.

Lemar was embarrassed, but he quickly reassured her, "Ainsley is a bit of a recluse who struggles with social gatherings, but he was anxious to meet you when I told him to come and see you in person today." Meshel's head rocked backwards, "oh-really Lemar? Don't act like you're doing me any favors." Lemar continued his plea, "At least he came out to meet you. Most times, he would refuse to leave home to see anybody. My Aunt even gets mad at him because he refuses to come to see her in person whenever she's in town and stops by."

"And I'm supposed to feel thrilled after Mr. Man ran off to his wife right after saying two words to me?" Meshel was insulted by Ainsley's attitude; she was not going to let Lemar off the hook.

"I know Meshel, but unfortunately, that's who he is. You know, it's family. Gotta love them, right?" As Lemar spoke he rubbed her shoulders, appealing to her softer side, hoping she would mercifully release him from her hook of dismay. *Ainsley should be better at this by now; he has a wife!* Lemar thought, feeling so disappointed as his brother let him down.

A few minutes after Ainsley's swift departure, mother Viola calls Lemar's cell phone. "It's my mom." He said to Meshel, then answered, "Hey, Ma."

"Hey, son, how's it going with Ainsley and Meshel finally meeting up?"

Lemar took a deep breath…, "Well, it was short. Ainsley did his usual, 'hi-and-bye!' He said he had to rush home to Cheyenne, now you know she keeps him on a tight leash?" Meshel could hear Viola's voice on the other end even though Lemar had the phone to his ear and off speaker.

"Yeah, that's my Ainsley. I wish he were more like Anton. I don't know where he gets it from. He's afraid to interact with new people; thank goodness for my daughter-in-law Cheyenne. She must inspire him, because I don't know how he convinced her to marry him. Speaking of marriage, are you and Meshel thinking about getting married?" Viola really hoped Lemar wouldn't marry Meshel, but probed Lemar for information just so that she could be ahead of the game.

At the sound of the word 'marriage,' Lemar almost bent his index-finger backward, pressing the phone tighter into his ear, just in case Meshel could hear his mother's voice. "Uhm, I'm thinking about it, Ma." He replied, sounding casual as if the subject wasn't an uncomfortable discussion at the moment; he was desperately trying to hide his fear of the subject from Meshel.

Lemar pressed the phone so hard against his ear that he nearly sprained his finger, as he tried to keep Meshel from hearing his mother's voice. It was too late. Meshel overheard Viola's inquiry about marriage, so she smiled to herself, letting him sweat it out as his mother dropped fire into his ear. That's right, Lemar, put a ring on it. Tell him, Ms. Viola! she thought. Meshel stared at Lemar, looking as if she couldn't hear the actual conversation; she tilted her head, signaling her thoughts to him. What is she trying to say to you?

Lemar felt the pressure caught between Meshel's intense stares and his mother's voice over the phone. Soon, he felt obligated to end the call with his mother, Viola. He immediately channeled his brother Ainsley's attitude, unwilling to discuss his emotions on the topic. He quickly asserted, "BYE, MA!" As he abruptly hung up! It was a bit too late, and Meshel was already aware, so she intended to press his buttons on the issue of marriage.

"And?" Meshel asked with her head still tilted to the side, unwilling to let Lemar off the hook again, that easily.

"And what, Luv? Lemar responded.

"And, marriage, that's what?" Meshel pushed back.

"Uhm, nothing. She just wanted to know when we were getting married," Lemar fearfully shared with Meshel.

"Hmmm. Okay," Meshel replied as she thought, When is he going to put a ring on my finger? She stared and smirked at Lemar, nodding slowly as she squinted her eyes at him. I've got my eye on you, mister. Let's see what you do.

CHAPTER 47

THE CONFESSION

The next day, after Lemar dropped Meshel off at work with a kiss, she kept thinking about the phone conversation between him and his mother. The fact that mother Viola even discussed marriage with Lemar, which was surprising for Meshel because mother Viola didn't get to spend as much time with her granddaughters anymore. I know I would be an excellent wife to Lemar, and I only need his trust. I wish he would ignore his past marital failure and learn from it, just like I learned from mine. She was deep in thought; meanwhile, Nellie was early for her shift and walked into the room to see her co-worker and friend lost in thought.

"Meshel? Meshel!" Nellie spoke louder, trying to get her attention.

"Oh, Hi, Nellie." Meshel finally replied as she gathered herself, feeling somewhat exposed and embarrassed. "You're early. How come?" She asked Nellie as she adjusted herself in her chair.

"Girl, my husband is at it again. He got mad at me for no reason. He accused me of cheating on him again, and I was at work this time. Thanks to you, you know how I've slowed down on sleeping around. I left home early before things got out of hand. I'm tired of his insecurities and just need to get away right now." Nellie admitted Meshel inspired her to be better in her marriage, but she was still sneaky in practice.

Meshel briefly remembered Nellie's attempted 'sexcapade' with Lemar. She and Nellie spoke about it and Nellie apologized.

"I knew I was out of bounds, but yeah, he turned me down. Good for you Meshel, you got the prize." She said, mocking Meshel. That conversation ended as Meshel told Nellie, "Lemar won't be giving you a ride anymore, and you certainly won't be riding him!" *Yeah, no rides here for you girl!* Meshel thought, drifting back into deep thoughts again.

Nellie was a bit flustered; she just bared her soul to Meshel and felt like Meshel just totally ignored her. "Meshel! Are you listening to me? I said I was wrong before, but I just hate being ignored."

Meshel heard Nellie, then quickly came back to reality and asked, "Oh my gosh! Did he hit you again, Nellie?"

"No, he didn't. I left before it got that far. But enough about me and my drama. How are you and Lemar doing?"

"Girl, let me tell you. Lemar's mother called him on his cell phone right after I met his rude brother Ainsley, and she asked him, "are you and Meshel thinking about getting married?"

"What? Meshel, you're kidding. How did he react?" Nellie had to sit down; she was shocked as she listened to Meshel's drama. It was way better gossip than the news of her and her husbands near fight at home.

"Well, first, he got nervous and tried to hide his mother's voice from me. He pressed the phone against his ear, so I just looked him directly in his eyes as he spoke to her. Then he damn near hung the phone up on her; all I heard was, "BYE, MA!" And click! Meshel and Nellie both burst into laughter at the same time. They both caught their breath, Meshel continued. "So then I pushed his buttons to make him admit what his mother said over the phone. His response was, 'She just wanted to know when we were getting married.'" Meshel said, mocking Lemar's masculine voice with her own tone. Then I said, 'Hmm, okay."

"Really, Meshel?" Nellie was jealous and sounded doubtful of Meshel's story.

Meshel was annoyed by Nellie's disbelief. "You act like you never had someone who truly loved you, and all you do is cheat and then blame the man for everything."

"Meshel, why did you have to go there? I never told you about the first man that proposed to me when I was younger, did I?"

"First proposal?" Meshel was stunned, now it was her turn to listen.

"When I was seventeen years old, I got pregnant. My boy-friend at the time was twenty-five, but he was way after my first boyfriend, that had dumped me for my best friend. This guy wanted to marry me. He told me he wanted to talk to my parents about it. You know?... He wanted to do the right thing by me? I told him no; I don't want my parents to find out. I felt like I was too young to get married, I was just having some fun with him. I told him I wanted to have an abortion instead." Nellie paused as she looked at Meshel's shocked open-eyed reaction.

She continued, "He was shocked, just like you are right now, but I didn't care. My first boyfriend and best friend did me wrong, and I swore I wouldn't let anyone get to me like that again. He begged me to keep the baby, told me he would work hard, and wanted us and the baby to be a family. But my mind was made up. I wanted an abortion, so he paid for me to have an abortion at one of the best clinics. He paid for my medications and ensured I had everything I needed to be taken care of. I healed up and wanted to return to having sex with him again like before. He was the first man to give me that feeling, but he refused to have sex with me again. He told me, 'I don't want this to happen again. So, this ends now. I wish you all the best. Take care.' He broke up with me!"

"That was your chance, girl," Meshel said, saddened though further disgusted after hearing Nellie's story.

"Yeah, I wish I had married him. That man truly loved me, and I was young and stupid, and that first feeling of ecstasy was all I cared about. I was more upset that he rejected me. Oh well!

CHAPTER 48

MR. MUSIC

Lemar's passion for music still drove him to his first onstage performance. So after many years, he spoke with Meshel about it, and she was highly supportive. "Yes, babe, I'll go with you. You should never give up on your passions." She said, knowing that her man was full of many talents.

He checked with his friends and found out there was a weekly open mic talent show for rap performers in Lower Manhattan. Meshel was his ride-or-die partner, but at this stage of their lives, it was just for fun, nothing more. They arrived a little early, and as they approached the doors to the venue, they were immediately noticed, especially Meshel because of her voluptuous figure.

Three rappers belonging to the same group were standing just outside the doors. They heckled everyone as they entered the building. They were tipsy from drinking alcohol. The sight of sexy Meshel with Lemar incited a reaction of jealousy. Lemar had words with them as he escorted Meshel safely through the glass doors. The bouncer inside the doors observed the skirmish and asked, "Are they out there talking their sh#! again?"

"Yeah, they are," Lemar answered. Both he and Meshel were annoyed, but they kept calm, remembering they were parents with children at home.

As the bouncer respectfully and professionally scanned them both with his metal detector wand, Meshel opened her Dior purse for his visual inspection for weapons. He informed them that "last week, the same trio insulted an entire crew of rappers, numbering about fifteen in total; they could have been beaten up really badly, we had to step outside and break the whole thing up. I guess they don't learn. You, folks, enjoy yourselves and try not to let them ruin your evening."

Lemar paid their cover charge as they entered the venue. As they walked in, they bee-lined straight for the bar to order refreshments. Then they left the bar behind, to sign up for Lemar's performance. The neon lights on both walls guided them to an open floor area in front of the stage. The DJ played different cuts of current music, meanwhile, at center stage there was a mic stand with a microphone on display for performers. Lemar's eyes beamed in on the Shure-SM57-wireless-microphone. He was excited because this tool was for his element, rapping.

Through the dimly lit scene, Meshel could still see Lemar's excitement. She was happy for him and saw the passion in his eyes as he beamed in on the microphone. He was hungry for this opportunity to showcase his talent.

Lemar clutched her hand as he performed in his head, nodding to the same music in mind that he gave to the DJ on his thumb drive for his turn on stage. As his focus intensified, trouble lurked closer toward himself and Meshel. The trio of rappers with whom he had words earlier finally made their way back into the club, the tallest and largest of the three stood right next to Lemar. They had entered much earlier to sign in to perform, then went outside for their usual shenanigans; heckling and intimidating any other fearful rappers that could possibly out-perform them.

Lemar put his back against the wall to cut off options if the adversary attacked. He shook Meshel's hand to get her attention. She saw the big fellow next to Lemar. Lemar looked around for the other two miscreants. They were on the other side of the club; they seemed entranced by the vibe of the music and current performers onstage. But it was apparent that the big fellow wanted to get his share of Lemar's attention. While watching 'big man' from the corner of his eye, Lemar told Meshel to go off and stand next to the show's host for safety. Meshel resisted at first, wanting to stand with her man, but Lemar calmly insisted she move for safety and take cover. Meshel's presence next to the host was not ignored. He knew the rapper-trio were troublemakers and had been watching them since their entry.

Lemar was not very tall but had a stocky build and broad shoulders. The host sensed the tension brewing and decided to call it back into order before it got out of hand. "Big man!" He said ironically to Lemar, "Take it easy." That also indicated to the 'big-fellow' that Lemar was ready for action. Lemar looked at his adversary eye-to-eye. The other two rappers were oblivious and stayed on the other side of the club, still preoccupied with the vibe of the music. The big-fellow saw in Lemar's eyes that he had no fear of him, and Lemar's position against the wall was geared for defense and offense, smart training. There were no further words exchanged between Lemar and 'big-fellow,' then the big-fellow broke off staring at Lemar and walked over to his two partners-in-rhyme. The trio were set to go onstage next after the current act.

Lemar walked over to the host, who stood near the base of the stage. He loved to watch the performances from the audience's point of view. Meshel still stood next to the host. "Big man, you alright?" He asked Lemar.

"Yeah, I'm good," Lemar replied, giving the host eye contact with a respectful nod of thanks. "You okay, Luv?" He asked Meshel.

"Yes, I'm fine. Those assholes!" She said as she clutched her Dior purse and Lemar's hand once again.

Lemar looked again at the trio of fellows on the other side of the club, and they were all collectively caught up in their own vibe. They were next to perform onstage.

"Big man. You were next after them, but I'm going to switch you with another performer. I don't want you all to cross each other onstage. Alright?" Said the host.

"No problem. Sounds good." Lemar replied, nodding once again, showing respect to his host.

Lemar and Meshel backed away from the stage to a more obscure part of the club as the trio of rappers stepped onstage to begin their performance. Lemar took the opportunity to call his friend Ben on his cell phone. He told Ben where he was with Meshel and what had happened outside and inside the club. Ben lived close by in Harlem. He told Lemar, "Say no more. I'm on my way right now. You know I stay healthy."

Lemar, feeling partially reassured, said a private prayer for protection for Meshel, himself, Ben and everyone in the club. He listened as the trio continued their performance. They sounded good, but Lemar was in another mindset and was in no mood to give them any admiration, not even privately for himself.

Time expired for the trio's performance, but they refused to get off the stage. They insisted they had more songs to perform. The host was now very annoyed, as he had a show to run, and these idiots were messing with his flow. The next performers were already positioned to get onstage, and the crowd was appalled at the trio's lack of decorum. The night's activities were stalled.

Lemar and Meshel looked at one another. Lemar was concerned for Meshel's safety. "I think we should leave if this continues." He said as he held Meshel's hand under the table. Meanwhile, he observed everyone in the club. Boos were heard from the audience. The rap trio resisted leaving the stage until the boos became unanimous around the entire club. The bouncers entered the stage area, and right behind them, Lemar's friend Ben walked in. Ben was built just as stocky as Lemar, only much taller.

There was no room for chit-chat as Ben acknowledged Lemar and Meshel through eye contact and a simple head nod. Then he posted himself next to their table as Lemar stood up to join him on alert. Meshel remained seated at the table, purse clutched, as the men prepared for any outcome, which included running outside as a first option.

The bouncers handled the trio, quickly grabbing and expelling the first two from the venue as the host reclaimed control of the event. The host then announced their departure, marking the end of their 'last welcomed' visit. The third big-fellow of course resisted being grabbed, but in the end was still manhandled by two bouncers and ousted to the street outside. They welcomed the opportunity to flex their skills and their authority. "Leave and don't come back in here! You guys are permanently banned from this venue!" They were told as the third fellow was pushed out to join his dusty team. The trio was then told by the police, who were already outside, to go home or face a cold jail cell for the night. They collected themselves in their state of drunken-embarrassment and left, stumbling as they walked away with a trail of choice words for the club and its patrons.

Ben followed the bouncers outside as they expelled the last of the trio, just to see firsthand what was taking place. Lemar remained at the table with Meshel to secure her safety. "They got kicked out," Ben said, as he returned and explained that he was also friends with one of the bouncers. "Don't worry about it,

Lem, just do your thing on that stage!" Let them hear that positive vibe that you possess, my brother." Ben and Lemar had met while Lemar was working on a job assignment in Harlem. The two found out they had a lot in common despite having different backgrounds.

The DJ cued Lemar's music for his song, 'They Call Me Down.' Lemar's act was ready to begin at the sound of the lead synthesizers, orchestral chords, and drums. His chorus was sung by a baritone singer that sounded similar to the singer Dennis Edwards:

Don't know, If I'll make it back home. Yes, I'm down.
Don't know, If I'll make it back home. They call me down.
I'm gonna stay, dooown dooown. What up, down?
I'm gonna stay, dooown dooown. I'm just stuck here in a dream.

The audience loved the chorus; now Lemar only had to deliver a worthy verse:

Yo! Desperados push my motto through the open plains.
How I'm gon' make it through this desert, for better days?
I ain't for following, Hollow man's an open frame.
Y'all know my Mission revision is like the middle name.
It's hot griddle; I fiddle around your riddling,
Diddly doing diddling. And no, I'm not belittling.

I'm sitting in the middle with cats who never fiddle.
And a little goes a long way, right man? The strong way
Seeking the prize like the big bad wolf
The wolverine pushing knowledge 'cause the status is proof.
Never fear, just beware from poison pies I puke.
Lion King with the ring, a fist holding the truth.
This maze in the night, this rap race ain't getting better.
Alpha Omega gon' get ya, that's why I'm not a sweater.
So what you telling me now? See, are you slavery bound?
It's Mickey Mic in your town; that's why They Calling Me Down

Back to the chorus, the crowd was elated, even admiration from some of the other performers. The host was pleased with the positive vibe of Lemar's music and content. It was different. It was refreshing.

Oooh, get 'em, babe, Meshel thought as she rocked her hips to his music and her man's performance. This was one of her favorite songs, and she also requested he make it the first song in his act. After two more songs, Lemar finished making his first impression on the audience. They gave him a round of cheers, applause and finger whistles. Job well done! He thanked the audience and blessed the host for creating opportunities for performers. Lemar, Ben, and Meshel made their way toward the exit. It was time to leave.

Lemar thanked Ben for showing up. "It's all love. You know

we're family." Ben responded. "Take this lovely lady home, and we'll catch up tomorrow, Lem. I have some business to handle back uptown." Lemar and Ben exchanged crossing forearms as their handshake and a hug before they parted for their respective vehicles. Meshel was glowing at her man, her knight in shining armor, she smiled all the way as Lemar drove them home.

Lemar was moved deeply that night by all that happened. As he drove through the local streets of Manhattan heading towards the West Side Highway, he made his decision by the time he stopped at the last traffic signal before entering the highway. He glanced over at Meshel; she smiled lovingly back at him. He thought to himself, Time to settle down and start this blended family. As he drove off with windows open to catch the view of the Hudson River and the night lights of New Jersey on the other side of the river, he thought, *I'm going to marry this woman.*

CHAPTER 49

THE PROPOSAL

Meshel took notice of her sisters and some of her friends. They were throwing shade at her relationship with Lemar. She struggled, finding no encouragement as she shared details about her relationship with many friends and family. Instead, she defended the growing pace of her and Lemar's love. She battled with complaints from her sisters about her lack of time for them. Nellie kept telling her, "I don't know why you just don't continue to date. You should always explore your options."

"But Lemar is a decent guy. Why would I need to look any further?" Meshel responded.

Nellie agreed but still argued, "Yeah, but you still shouldn't settle for the first nice guy." As if she wanted to live vicariously through Meshel and snatch away her man at the same time too.

"Nah, I'm good," Meshel replied, shutting Nellie down. Now she was seeing right through Nellie's deceitful plots.

Between her sisters and her friends, Meshel could find no one that genuinely celebrated or shared her happiness about Lemar being in her life. Pamela and Estelle witnessed her pain and dissatisfaction with both of her sons' fathers. They thought Lemar was a bit too much to be true, so they didn't want Meshel to throw caution to the wind and commit so soon.

Meshel listened to everyone but was determined to give Lemar a fair chance. She wanted to enjoy their love and be free to share her enthusiasm with the people she cared for. However, for some odd reason, there seemed to be a hint of resentment and, at times, splashes of jealousy. Although her sisters were married and seemed happy with their husbands, the decision of marriage was ultimately hers to make, and Lemar's.

Mother Viola thought her time with her granddaughters was diminished as Meshel spent more time with them. Viola often popped up unannounced at Lemar's house, especially if the twins were there with Meshel. She often tried to undercut Meshel's presence in front of the twins; that disrespect became a point of contention between Lemar and his mother. "Mom, they are fine. Meshel is perfectly capable of taking care of them; no, she is not trying to take Kim's place or yours. But she does have her own role to play with them." Lemar told his mother.

Kim was still somewhat angry at Lemar. Although it had been some years since their divorce, she somehow kept in contact with Mother Viola. The two secretly conspired to break up Lemar and Meshel's relationship so that they could have 'their preferences' prevail in his life.

Through her ex-husband and Marcus' father, Charlston Boyd, Aunt Thea, Meshel's in-law criticized Meshel as she thought it was too soon to introduce a new man to Marcus and Ashton.

Despite all the negativity, Lemar and Meshel could not keep away from each other, nor their hands off each other.

Lemar's cousin Royce was still a profound influence on him; Royce became concerned for his younger cousin, a single man who was only getting older. His advice to Lemar was simple:

"Cuz, you don't want to get old with no one by your side, just look at your parents. They're both single." Lemar was stumped, rendered silent by Royce's words. It made him think hard. It made him think deeply. Having love in my life is important, but besides the love of my relatives, the love of a trustworthy woman is paramount.

He truly loved Meshel. She was pretty, naturally witty, kind to a fault, innocent in some ways, and sexy to boot; plus she loved him. She said it first, which she never let him forget. Occasionally she ribbed Lemar, "you were too much of a punk to say, 'I love you.' So I said it first, remember that, okay?"

Lamar felt she was his 'genuine article,' so after that night at the club, he started shopping for the perfect engagement ring to propose to his love, Meshel.

He had already given her Le Vien chocolate diamond earrings set in rose gold. *This would be the perfect theme for her engagement ring. I like the way it looks against her skin ton*e, he thought. He found the right ring at the jewelry store and planned to surprise Meshel. This had to be special, memorable, and silence her quibbles about saying, 'I said I love you first.'

Lemar set a date for Meshel and himself to dine at the Negril Village-Jamaican cuisine restaurant in lower Manhattan. The food was famously delicious. Even the mayor of New York City at the time was a regular patron and supporter. It was Roland's recommendation. "By the way, I approve of you marrying my 'big-headed' sister. She needs a guy like you to take good care of her and keep her calm." Said Roland after choosing this excellent restaurant for Lemar to initiate his proposal to Meshel.

"Thanks, bro. I really appreciate this blessing from you." Lemar said.

They started with the Jamaican codfish fritters in honor of Meshel's love for Bajan fish cakes. Then they ordered separate entrees, intending to share their meals. Lemar ordered the delicious House Red Snapper with vegetables, while Meshel had their Tasting Plate so she could sample their Oxtails, Curry Goat, Jerk Chicken, Peas and Rice, Vegetables, and Plantains. They sipped on a glass of Rum Punch as they gazed into each other's eyes just before Lemar had his favorite grapenut ice cream for dessert. They were too full to eat the Sorrel Petals Cheesecake Meshel ordered for dessert, so they packed it to take it home with the rest of their entrees. Lemar needed to make some room for Meshel and some of her 'soft dessert.'

Secretly, Lemar had a bottle of champagne waiting at the house in the refrigerator. After just one deep sip of champagne, they devoured each other late into the night. Lemar awakened before Meshel. It was time to put his main plan into action. He gave her a light kiss on her forehead, remembering their night together, which left him even more excited about his proposal. She was sound asleep. Lemar took out the engagement ring and slipped it on her wedding ring finger. He put his arm around her to hug her, as he went back to sleep himself.

As the day dawned, Meshel awoke. At first, she looked at Lemar, she smiled after the night they had. She felt an object around her finger, so she looked at her hand. Shocked, she wondered to herself, Did Lemar put this ring on my finger? With excitement, she awakened Lemar. "Gooood morning, handsome!" she said.

"Good morning, Luv," replied Lemar.

Meshel started screaming, "ARE WE ENGAGED?" She asked Lemar.

"I guess we are!" Lemar replied, hoping that meant she accepted his yet unspoken proposal.

"Meshel. I find that you are a unique woman and a very special part of my life. I love the way you care for me and the way you care for the children in our lives. Would you do me the honor of being my wife."

"Thank you." Meshel said.

"That's unusual. 'Yes', usually goes with a proposal." Lemar commented.

As the tears trickled down Meshel's cheeks, she responded, "I said 'thank you' because you decided to trust me to be your partner for life, and you know I'm going to take care of you, and I know you will do the same for me."

Lemar was astonished by her response, they began kissing to

celebrate the new development in their lives.

The wedding was an elegant affair in a white mansion on a light snowy winter evening. The ceremony was officiated by Matthew Jones, Lemar's mentor and guide.

THE END

VIZIER VAUGHN

A product of Caribbean ancestry and New York City living, Vizier Vaughn fused his two cultures, guided by his faith, which tempered his insight, wisdom, and life experiences.

His curiosity to understand the world we live in drives his thirst for knowledge. Vizier finds his inspiration for writing from the stories and experiences of his life and his observation of the world around him.

Vizier Vaughn has a very diverse academic background, which he draws from and weaves into his writing and character building. His academic resume includes studies in the areas of liberal arts, mechanical engineering, computer science and information technology, multimedia development and management, and business administration. Vaughn's passion for writing began while studying Multimedia Design and Management at the

College of Westchester where an English professor led him to hone in on his love for writing. With the guidance of his English professor, Vaughn enhanced his writing skills and developed his craft of sentence structure and storytelling.

Vaughn embraces his spirituality and lives his life with integrity. He is a firm believer in Jesus Christ whose teachings have set the standard for the morals and values he lives by. He also credits his spiritual, historical, and sociological knowledge and wisdom to his mentor of over thirty years.

The name Vizier Vaughn pays homage to Vaugn's role with his friends; it means, "the little-one that will give great advice!"